THE CONTRACT WITH THE BILLIONAIRE

A FAKE MARRIAGE SERIES BOOK 3

MARIE MEYER

Created with Vellum

To Megan Ruff

You made it through the first book I ever wrote and helped me become the writer I am today.

CHAPTER ONE

LILLIAN STOOD in front of her bed, staring down at the satin button-up shirt and sharp, black pencil skirt that Tamara had lent to her. She reached out and ran her hand across the smooth fabric. Anxiety rose up in her gut, and she placed her hand on her stomach.

She had to get this job. It was her last hope.

She let her fingers linger on the bulge underneath her slip. It was becoming more pronounced—the fifth month of pregnancy would do that to a woman. She just hoped it wasn't *that* obvious. A new employer would most likely frown upon a pregnant woman, and she was running out of time and options.

Tears stung her eyelids as she let the memories of her previous pregnancy wash over her. If this pregnancy was anything like that one, she needed medical insurance. Now.

Letting out a deep sigh, she slipped out of her robe and

dressed, sucking in her stomach as she zipped up the side of her skirt. Thankfully, it didn't split once it was up, although it felt like it might. And that would be just her luck, her reaching out to shake billionaire Reed Williamson's hand just to have her zipper explode.

She slipped on the blouse and, as her fingers did the last button, she swallowed her fear. She wasn't going to think like that today. She was going to be calm and confident. There was no way she could let her potential employer know she was hanging onto her sanity by a thread. That her life was falling apart and there was nothing she could do to piece it back together.

There was a soft knock on the door. Lillian let out her breath—hoping to calm her nerves—and forced a smile.

"Come in," she said as she sat down on the bed and slipped her feet into her shoes.

The door opened, revealing Tamara standing there. She was in her signature scrubs and ponytail. She had a bowl of cereal in her hand, and her lips were moving as she chewed. Her gaze swept over Lillian, and she dropped her jaw in an exaggerated movement. Tamara was back from her week-long shift as one of the nurses for billionaire and business tycoon, George Williamson—Reed's grandfather.

"Geez, you look better in my clothes than I do," she said, stepping into the room and walking over to collapse on the ratty armchair in the corner.

"I do not," Lillian said, standing up and brushing down the front of her skirt. "Can you see it?"

It. Not "baby"—it. After she lost her first baby at twenty-five weeks, she couldn't bear to acknowledge this one. What if the same thing happened? She wasn't sure her heart could take another loss.

"Ugh, no. You always look amazing, even when you're pregnant. I don't look half as good, and I've got no excuse." Tamara took another bite of cereal. "Joshua's an idiot," she said through gritted teeth.

"Let's not go there today. I'm already nervous as it is." Lillian raised her hand. The last thing she needed to be talking about was her ex-husband, Mr. Run at the First Sign of Stress. He hadn't wanted the previous pregnancy, and when he found out they were pregnant again, he told her to either abort the baby or he'd be gone. He moved out the next day, and they were divorced within the month. He didn't bother giving away his parental rights, making a snide comment about how it didn't matter; she couldn't keep a baby inside anyway.

Now she was all alone, with no family around. And pregnant. Anxiety crept back into her chest. She swallowed, trying to push her emotions down. Not today. She had to get a grip.

Tamara nodded. "You're right. We don't need to waste any more energy on that loser." She shot Lillian a comforting smile. "You shouldn't be worried. You're going to rock this interview. Mr. Billionaire Bachelor is going to love you."

"I still can't believe you got me this interview," Lillian

said as she made her way over to her dresser and picked up her heart locket necklace.

Tamara hesitated, and then shrugged. "He owed me a favor. After all, I do take care of his grandfather."

"Which translates to, you eavesdrop on private conversations and use that information for your own personal gain." Lillian shot a glance over at Tamara, who had an incredulous look on her face.

"I do not. That would be unethical. However, if said people were talking a bit too loud, and I just happened to overhear"—she raised her hands—"it's not my fault."

Lillian couldn't help but smile. Tamara was always the strong, outspoken one in the friendship. Always getting them into private functions or getting free drinks at the bar.

She slipped her pearl earrings on and then turned. "Well, I am grateful. If I get this job, it will be a godsend."

Tamara had finished her cereal and placed the bowl next to her chair. She stood and was across the room in a few strides. "You're going to be just fine." She pulled Lillian into a hug.

"Thanks," Lillian said as emotion coated her throat. It had been a hard year and a half. She was grateful to have Tamara by her side, guiding her through it. Now, more than ever, she needed a friend. Someone to help her. She doubted she could function without her best friend by her side.

"Alright, enough blubbering. Get going. You're going be late," Tamara said as she stepped back and waved toward the door.

Butterflies erupted in Lillian's stomach as she grabbed her purse. "Are you sure I can do this?" She took a small step.

Tamara linked arms with her. "I know you can. But, if you don't hurry, you're going to be late. And I'm pretty sure Mr. Williamson will not be too happy with that."

Lillian took a deep breath. She could do this. She knew she could. Once she was in the hallway of her rundown apartment complex, she had an overwhelming desire to vomit. But she muscled it down, blaming it on the pregnancy instead of her out-of-control nerves.

When she stepped out of her building and onto the sidewalk, she felt better. The sun was out and the sides of the building glowed with sunshine. People rushed past her, and she had to spin to keep from getting trampled.

The fresh air helped settle her stomach during the fifteen-minute ride into New York City. It wasn't until she was stepping out of the cab that the nausea hit again. Williamson Plaza stretched up toward the sky, like a beacon. Lillian felt tiny, standing in its shadow.

"Are you going, lady?" the cab driver's pronounced Brooklyn accent snapped her back to reality.

"Yeah," she said as she reached into her purse and pulled out a twenty. After she slammed the door, the cab driver took off, leaving her alone. She took in an uneasy breath, and turned to face the steps in front of her.

You can do this, she chanted in her head. *Reed Williamson is going to hire you.* Her foster mom was always talking about positive self-talk and how amazing it was. Even though Lillian always wrote it off as hippie talk, at this moment, she was willing to try anything.

She pulled open the tall, tinted-glass doors and stepped into the lobby. Men and women in tailored suits moved around her. She was grateful that she'd borrowed Tamara's clothes. She would have felt completely out of place in her clay-stained ones.

Lillian made it past the security guard and over to the elevators without tripping or doing something equally embarrassing. She was not used to wearing heels, and she hoped that it wasn't evident to everyone around her. She reached out and pressed the up button of the elevator. The doors opened, and she boarded.

The ride up to the thirtieth floor felt like an eternity. Lillian kept her gaze on her shoes as she counted the chimes that sounded as the elevator passed each floor.

Finally it stopped, and the doors slid open. Lillian peered out to see a woman with a tight bun wearing a leopard-print dress with a plunging neckline, sitting at a desk in front of her. She had a phone's receiver pressed between her shoulder and ear. Every so often, she'd sigh and then mumble something.

The floor was made of white marble and a couch with a matching set of armchairs was positioned on the far wall. The whole room felt so sterile. So formal. This was not where Lillian belonged.

Comprehensive health insurance, Lillian repeated to

herself as she plastered on a smile and approached the receptionist. The doors of the elevator closed behind her, stranding her on the thirtieth floor.

When she approached the desk, the woman didn't look up. It wasn't until Lillian cleared her throat that the woman's gaze flicked over to her. She raised one perfectly manicured eyebrow as if to ask, *what are you doing here?*

"I have a meeting with Mr. Williamson," Lillian said.

The receptionist ran her gaze over Lillian, and then turned her attention to the computer in front of her. She said a few "uh-huhs" as she clicked the keys.

Before the receptionist told her what to do, a side door opened and a woman stepped out. Her white hair was cut in a short A-line bob. She had speckled glasses perched on the tip of her nose and a red scarf that accented her dark suit.

A relieved expression passed over her face as she approached Lillian. "I'm so happy you're here. I was worried that you weren't going to come."

Lillian parted her lips. Who was this woman? And they'd been expecting her, specifically? That seemed strange. The job as personal assistant to a billionaire had to be an in-demand job. Surely, there had been a ton of applicants.

"Bonnie Williamson," she said, extending her hand.

Lillian studied it for a moment before she reached out and shook Bonnie's hand. Williamson. Was she related to Reed Williamson?

Before Lillian could ask, Bonnie dropped her hand and

waved for her to follow. "Did the agency fill you in on what we need?" she asked, peering over her shoulder as she led Lillian past the receptionist and through the glass door that said Williamson Investments.

Lillian leaned forward. "Agency?"

Bonnie nodded. "The person who sent you."

Did she mean Tamara?

Before she could answer, Bonnie waved her hand. "Never mind. Client confidentiality. We told them to keep it hush hush so I'm sure they didn't tell you everything." Bonnie paused outside of a glass door that led to a conference room.

A man in a dark blue suit sat at the far end of the table. He had round glasses and greying hair. He was flipping through some papers in front of him. Lillian felt Bonnie's gaze on her as she rested her hand on Lillian's shoulder.

"I know this is all crazy, but it's for the best. I just can't wait until this is all over," she said as she reached out and pulled on the large brass door handle.

As they stepped into the room, the man at the table glanced up. He set his pen down and stood.

"Mrs. Williamson," he said, buttoning his suit coat. When his gaze fell on Lillian, he nodded. "Ma'am."

"This is Orson Coswell. He'll be dealing with the contract," Bonnie said as she motioned toward a chair and then sat in the one next to it.

"Contract?" Wow, they were serious about their employees here at Williamson's Investments. Wait. Did this mean she got the job? "I'm hired?" Lillian asked. Her heart began to race. Was this a dream? She reached out and pinched her leg. A sharp pain raced through her. Well, she was awake.

"Hired?" Bonnie chuckled. "Well, I guess you could say that. Although we'd like to classify it more as you joining our family." She patted the tabletop in front of her. "It's all for Reed and the betterment of this company."

Orson nodded. He'd returned to his chair and placed his pen on top of the papers in front of him. "Now, this is your basic contract. It says you agree to stay with Mr. Williamson for at least a year, or until he is promoted to CEO. Also, there is a confidentiality clause in here. Basically, if you go to the press with any information, we'll..." He glanced up at her. "Just don't talk about anything you see or hear."

Lillian stared at Orson. That sort of made sense. She was probably going to be privy to a lot of information about Reed and Williamson Investments. A high-profile company like this had to have a lot of secrets. But there was one part that she couldn't quite figure out. Why did she have to stay as a personal assistant until Reed became CEO? She parted her lips to ask, but Bonnie spoke before she could say anything.

"The income is $100,000 a year with a parting bonus of $250,000. Plus, all expenses paid. Insurance, a place to live, and a clothing stipend. If you're going to be seen next to Reed, you need to look the part," Bonnie said, tapping her fingers as she spoke.

Lillian almost swallowed her tongue. Never in her life had she ever imagined she would be offered that much money. "I, well—" She couldn't form coherent sentences, so she decided to pinch her lips shut and nod.

Bonnie studied her. "Did you want more?"

Lillian's eyes widened. Not wanting to jinx this, she just shook her head. "No. What you said will be fine."

Bonnie tapped the table to get Orson's attention. "Add another hundred thousand to the bonus."

Lillian raised her hand. "No, no. That's okay. I'm sure I'll be just fine with a"—her voice dropped to a whisper —"quarter million."

Bonnie studied her. "Well, if you do a good job, I will include more when this is over."

Lillian nodded. "That seems fair."

Orson pushed the papers in her direction and indicated where she should sign. After what felt like the fiftieth signature, he declared that she was finished, gathered up the papers, and left. Lillian sat back in her chair with her head spinning. What had just happened? How had she gotten this lucky?

Was fate finally smiling down on her?

Bonnie stood and motioned for her to follow. "I guess it's time to meet Reed."

Lillian nodded as she pushed back her chair and stood. Out in the hall, Bonnie fell into step with her.

"Now, he's not going to be happy about you, or this arrangement, but it needs to happen," Bonnie said.

Lillian snapped her gaze over to Bonnie. Why wouldn't Reed be happy about her being his assistant? Tamara was pretty adamant that Reed had wanted to meet her, and that this arrangement would be advantageous for both of them. "Really? If it's going to be a problem, I can wait. He should probably interview me first." Panic rose up in her chest. She needed this job, and the last thing she wanted was to get her hopes up just to have them dashed when billionaire Reed Williamson waved her away.

Bonnie patted her arm. "Nonsense. That boy doesn't know what he wants. Sometimes, it takes a mother's guidance to help him see. He may feel that it's impossible to fulfill this stipulation, but I'm not ready to give up. Not yet."

Relief flooded Lillian. If she had the support of Bonnie, perhaps she would fight Reed to keep her.

They stopped at the door at the end of the hall, and Bonnie shot her what seemed like an encouraging smile. Then she raised her hand and knocked a few times.

"Come in," a deep, smooth voice said.

Bonnie reached out and grasped the door handle. Lillian held her breath as Bonnie pushed open the door.

"What do you want, Mom?" Reed asked.

"I'm here to introduce you to your wife."

Lillian's heart began to race. Had she heard Bonnie right? What did she just call her?

CHAPTER TWO

Reed leaned against the metal frame that supported the large picture windows in his office. The afternoon sun shone down on him, warming his already hot skin. Frustration coursed through his veins as he took a few deep breaths. He couldn't believe his grandfather. A marriage stipulation? Was he serious?

Reed deserved full ownership of Williamson Investments. Not Mason. He'd been the one carrying this company on his back since he graduated top of his class from Harvard Business School. And what had his philandering half-brother done? Nothing. But that didn't seem to matter to their grandfather. He needed to marry, or Mason would get full control of the company.

Reed scrubbed his face with his hand. The fact that George Williamson felt he could force him into matrimony was ridiculous. It was the most old-fashioned and backwards stipulation ever.

Reed pushed away from the window and made his way over to his desk. For the last week, he'd been counseling with Orson, the family lawyer, trying to find a way around this clause. But he couldn't come up with anything. If he didn't get married, he'd lose the title of CEO to Mason. Period.

Reed picked up a dart on his desk and readied it. He narrowed his eyes and stared at the center circle on the board eight feet away. Taking a deep breath, he let the dart soar.

It landed smack dab in the middle of the board. Bull's-eye.

Why did it have to be marriage? His grandfather was cruel. Reed's heart squeezed tight as he thought about Hannah. He'd found the girl that he wanted to love forever. But, just like every relationship in his life, it had come crashing down. Nothing like finding out that your fiancée was pregnant with your half-brother's baby. Now they were planning a wedding and a baby shower, and Reed had nothing. Not even a blip on the romance radar.

Reed picked up another dart as a wave of sadness washed over him. As much as he wanted to be over Hannah, he wasn't. It was hard with her still in his life. She still made his stomach turn inside out. He wanted to say it was because he hated her, but that was a lie. It felt like she would never leave him, even though six months had passed since she'd left. Why couldn't his heart understand that?

Wrestling down his feelings of self-pity, he dropped down onto his office chair and drummed the desk with his fingers. He needed to get his head on straight and do some work. He'd convince his grandfather that this was a ridiculous stipulation, he just needed to figure out how.

Just as he shook his mouse to wake up his computer, there was a knock on the door. Grateful for the distraction, Reed called out, "Come in."

The door opened, and he saw his mom peeking through the crack.

"What do you want, Mom?" He didn't have time for this. There was no way he wanted to go through another round of "you should get married, it's your responsibility."

His mom stepped into the room with an uneasy expression. This was never good.

"I'm here to introduce you to your wife." His mom stepped to the side to reveal a small red-head behind her.

Reed's ears rang as he blinked a few times. Had he heard her right? "Excuse me? Wife?"

When his gaze made its way over to his supposed wife, he saw that her eyes were as wide as saucers. She leaned over to his mom and whispered, "Um, what did you say? How are he and I married?"

His mom glanced down at her. "Didn't the agency talk to you?"

The woman's face paled. "I think you have me mistaken for someone else." She clutched her purse with one hand and braced her stomach as if she was about to be sick.

"You're not from Elite Soulmate Agency?"

Reed pushed back his chair and walked around his desk. This woman looked as if she was about to faint. He reached out his hand. "Come with me. Let's sit you down before you fall over and injure yourself."

The woman glanced down at his hand and then up to his face. For a moment, it looked as if she was about to protest but then pinched her lips shut and nodded.

Once he had her situated in the armchair across from his desk, he turned to his mom. She had wide eyes as her gaze kept slipping to the woman she'd brought in.

"What is going on?" he asked, stepping up to her.

She glanced over at him. "I don't know how that happened. I swear she said that she was with the agency. Didn't you say that Georgina sent you?"

The woman's eyes widened. "No. You didn't ask me that."

His mom made her way over to the chair next to hers and sat. "I swear you said that." Her brow furrowed. "Why would you let me go on and on if you weren't sent by the agency? Why would you sign the contract?"

The woman opened her purse and pulled out a bracelet. She put it on her wrist, pressing on a small button in the middle of the fabric. It was an anti-nausea bracelet. Reed had seen his grandmother use the same one.

"I thought you were talking about the personal assistant position I was here to interview for." Her gaze flicked over to

Reed, and he thought he detected a pink hue to her cheeks. Must be the nausea.

His mom pressed her hand against her forehead. "This is not good."

Feeling the need to step into this sinking ship of a situation, Reed walked over and leaned against his desk so he could face both women. He extended his legs out in front of him. "I'm sure this was just a simple mix-up. So she signed the contract, no big deal."

His mom's bright red lips were pinched together as she tried to muster a confident expression. "Yeah," she whispered, but a moment later she sprang from her chair. "I've got to call the agency and talk to Orson."

The sound of his office door closing filled the palpable silence. When Reed turned his attention back to the strange woman, he found that she was blotting her eyes with a tissue. Was she crying?

He felt bad for her. She was here hoping for a job, and got dragged into his mom's ridiculous schemes.

"Hey," he said as he grabbed the recently vacated armchair and pulled it closer to her. He reached out and let his hand hover over her arm. Would it seem supportive or just creepy? He went with creepy, so he leaned his elbows on his knees and clasped his hands in front of him. "It'll all be over in a minute."

The woman glanced over at him, her eyes were puffy. "So there's no job?"

He shook his head.

Her lip quivered as she dropped her gaze.

Whoops. He didn't mean to make her more upset. "Hey, but maybe that's a good thing. You've seen how crazy my family is. Most women run in the opposite direction of me."

She let out a laugh. "Yeah. I've heard that's a common plight among the wealthy."

If she only knew. Sure, women threw themselves at him, but he always struggled to know if they were there for him or for his money. And the last person he'd thought was genuine ended up in bed with his half-brother. So his track record was terrible.

"It's not all it's cracked up to be."

She sniffled and stuffed the tissue into her purse. "It's a lot better than what I've got going on." She took a deep breath and whispered something that sounded like, "I needed this."

When he leaned in, hoping to catch what she was saying, she just smiled and shouldered her purse. "Well, Mr. Williamson, I'll get out of your hair. I've got to dust off my job searching skills." She stood and started toward the door.

An idea formed in his mind as he watched her leave. How bad would it be if they continued with this ridiculous matchmaking debacle? It would save him from his mom attempting this again, and it seemed as if this woman could use it too.

"What did they offer you?" he asked as she reached out to turn the handle.

Her shoulders tightened and she slowly turned around. "$100,000 a year with a bonus at the end."

He let out a whistle. His mom definitely wasn't stingy with his money. "That's all?"

She wrung her hands. "And full benefits, a place to live, and a clothing stipend," she whispered.

He leaned back in his chair. "That's a pretty nice deal."

She nodded but then raised her hand as if to stop him. "Yes, but that's a crazy thing your mom is asking us to do. You don't want to be married to a complete stranger. After all, I could be a serial killer or something."

He stood and strolled over to her. He couldn't deny that she was cute. The way she kept tucking strands of her hair behind her ear, or the way her cheeks hinted pink every time he looked at her. She was intriguing.

When he was a foot away from her, he bent down to catch her gaze. "Are you a serial killer?"

Her eyes widened as she chewed her lower lip. "No." Then she leaned into him. "But that's what a serial killer would say when asked if they were a serial killer."

She was quirky and sweet, and he couldn't help but like her. There was something about her that drew him in. She wasn't like any of the women he'd met at galas or stuffy parties.

He extended his hand. Her gaze dropped to it and made its way back up to meet his.

"Reed Williamson." He wiggled his fingers, hoping that she wouldn't leave him hanging.

She hesitated and then met his gesture. "Lillian Brunette."

He shook her hand. "Well, Lillian, what do you say? Fake a marriage with me?"

Her eyes widened as she hesitated and then wriggled her hand from his grasp. "I can't," she whispered and reached behind her back to grab the door handle. "You don't want to get involved in my mess." She opened the door and moved to step out.

She yelped as she ran into Orson, who was standing just outside of the door with a stack of papers. He straightened his glasses as his gaze moved from Lillian over to Reed.

"We need to talk," he said.

Reed nodded and stepped out of the way so that Orson and Lillian could enter his office. A panicked look raced across Lillian's face as she glanced down the hallway and back to Orson.

"I should just go," she said. "You can probably shred the documents without me."

"Actually, Ms. Brunette, we can't. You'll need to hear this."

Her face paled as her gaze flicked over to Reed. "What does that mean?"

Orson situated himself on one of the armchairs and motioned toward the other. "You signed a non-disclosure agreement," he said as he shuffled through the paper. He said a quiet "ah" and then raised a sheet. "Right here." He pointed to a signature.

"Okay?" she asked.

"Well, Williamson Investments doesn't believe that if you walk out that door, you will keep what happened here a secret. You're a liability."

She shook her head. "What are you saying?"

"They think you'll auction off what you learned here today to the highest bidder," Reed said. He knew what Orson was saying. She'd signed a contract, and they weren't going to let that go. Inside he cursed his mom. Why had she done this?

Lillian glanced over at him. "But I didn't know what I was signing." She began to pace. "So, what? I have to stay married to Reed?" She waved her hand toward him.

His stomach twinged at her reaction. He wasn't that terrible. Was he?

"Yes. Until his grandfather declares that he has fulfilled his inheritance stipulation or passes away, you must remain married to Reed."

Her face fell. "And I have no say in the matter?"

He hated what this was doing to her. He'd make it right. "Of course you do. Orson, you're being ridiculous. Let this poor woman out of the contract." The last thing he wanted was to be married. Much less be married to a woman who didn't want to be married to him.

Orson shook his head. "I'm sorry, Reed. I don't work for you; I work for Williamson Investments. They own this contract. Until you are declared owner, you have no say."

He sighed. "The only person who can null this contract is your grandfather, but I'm guessing you don't want me to tell him what your mother attempted."

Reed ran his hand through his hair. No, he didn't want that. He shot Lillian a sheepish look. Would she do this for him?

Her expression turned serious. "And if I walk away?"

Orson shook his head. "You won't want to do that. You signed away all your assets. You'd be homeless and owe Williamson Investments the amount they promised to pay you."

Lillian fanned herself with her hand as she quickened her pace.

"Listen, I'm just the middle man. We thought we were hiring someone to play this part. We wanted to make sure that information wasn't leaked. We had to put that in the contract to protect Reed and this company." He gave them a smile. "I hope you understand."

Lillian just scoffed and kept pacing.

Orson straightened the stack of papers and laid them on Reed's desk. "They're ready for your signature as well," he said as he stood and made his way toward the door. Right before he left, he turned to Lillian. "This is a once in a lifetime opportunity. Take advantage of it. Reed's a great guy." He shot Reed a smile before slipping from the room.

Once he was gone, Reed turned his attention back to Lillian. "So," he said, trying to gauge her reaction.

She stopped and stared at her hands. Then she slowly glanced up at him. "I guess I have to pack up my apartment and tell my landlord."

He nodded. This whole situation was ridiculous, but he was willing to do whatever she needed. "I could call a service to do that. After all, you're marrying a billionaire."

Her lips parted as her jaw dropped slightly. Then she shook her head. "No. I can do this."

"Of course." He smiled over at her. "Don't worry, my apartment's nice."

She cleared her throat. "I'm going to be living with you?"

Heat boiled to the surface. What was he thinking? "I'm not sure. I'll have to read the contract. But knowing my mom, it's probably the case."

Her gaze moved toward the stack of paper. "Yeah. I should probably read it as well. Try to figure out what other things I committed myself to."

He nodded. "I'll bring a copy over to you."

She pulled the strap of her purse up higher on her shoulder. "I should go. If I don't, I might find myself contractually obligated to more." She turned and made her way out into the hall. Just as she disappeared, he realized that he didn't have her contact information. He followed after her.

"Hey, Lillian?" he called to her retreating frame.

She hesitated and then turned. "Yeah?"

"Leave your contact info with Persephanie at the front desk."

She glanced in the direction of the lobby and nodded.

When Reed was back in his office, he collapsed on his office chair and stared at the stack of papers in front of him. What just happened?

CHAPTER THREE

"Oh. My. Gosh," Tamara breathed as she stood in the middle of Lillian's room the next day. Her gaze darted around as she tried to process what Lillian had told her.

Stifling a sigh, Lillian pulled a shirt off its hanger and folded it up. She really wasn't sure what she was doing or what exactly had happened. Was she really marrying a billionaire? Just thinking those words made her feel ridiculous. She wanted to tell Tamara the truth, but with the non-disclosure agreement, mum was the word.

"It's really not a big deal," Lillian said as she shrugged.

Tamara's eyes widened. "But it's Reed Williamson. Are you serious? The job requires you live with him? Lucky," she whispered as she sunk onto Lillian's bed.

Lillian set the shirt in the suitcase that she'd perched on her bed and then turned her attention to her friend. "About that, how much do you know about this position? Like, what exactly did Reed's grandfather say?"

Tamara reached out and flicked the zipper to the suitcase with her finger. "It was more that I overheard a conversation from Reed's mom. She was on the phone talking to some agency about sending a girl to help assist Reed. I figured you could use the break, so I told you to go." She sighed as she leaned back, propping herself up with an extended arm. "Had I known how comprehensive this job was, I would have gone myself."

If she only knew how comprehensive it was. Lillian pinched her lips shut. There was no way she could spill the beans, especially to Tamara, who couldn't keep a secret. Lillian needed to distract herself. Turning, she grabbed another shirt from its hanger and set it in the suitcase.

"So, tell me about this elusive billionaire bachelor. Is he as handsome as they show in the magazines?" Tamara asked.

Lillian shot her an annoyed look. Fawning over a hot, rich guy was the last thing she needed to do. Not when she had the responsibility she did—even if she still wasn't ready to acknowledge its existence. "I didn't notice."

Except she had. Reed was handsome in an almost unworldly way. There was no way his chiseled jaw or deep brown eyes could have been created by accident. It was unfair to the rest of the male population. He was tall—over six feet— and he had this down-to-earth quality about him that mesmerized Lillian. She seemed to forget how to talk when she was around him.

Tamara snorted. "That's a lie."

"Is not."

"Yes, it is. I can see it in your eyes. You can never make eye contact when you're lying."

Lillian shot her friend an exasperated look and turned back to her suitcase. "I don't have time in my life for a man, and you know that."

"Because of the baby?"

At the mention of her pregnancy, Lillian's hand made its way to her stomach. What was she going to tell Reed—how had she forgotten this huge detail? "I'm not going to tell him because there will be no baby." Tears choked her throat as she remembered back to the horrid night a year ago. The night she lost the first baby.

"Lil, that doesn't happen all the time. This one is going to be different, and then what are you going to tell your boss?"

Heat raced to Lillian's cheeks as nausea flooded her body. She knew it was foolish to keep this a secret, but she couldn't bring herself to tell him or anyone else. She was jinxed in more ways than one. Right now, she needed to keep her head down and do her job. That way, Reed couldn't fire her if he found out. "I'm going to be sick," she said as she beelined for the armchair in the far corner and collapsed on it.

Tamara was next to her in a second, grabbing her wrist and counting her heartbeat.

Lillian rolled her eyes. "What are you doing?"

Tamara pursed her lips in a silent *shush*. Then she focused on her watch as she bobbed her head. A minute passed before she dropped Lillian's arm.

"Your pulse seems fine."

Lillian stared at her. "Of course it's fine. I told you I was going to be sick, not have a heart attack."

Tamara patted her hand, made her way back over to the bed, and plopped down. "Just wanted to make sure you're not dehydrated."

Lillian's stomach began to settle, so she stood. "If I am, it's because my best friend is making her pregnant friend pack by herself in an eighty-degree apartment." The summer was brutal, and in a poorly ventilated apartment, it was even worse.

Tamara shot her a sympathetic look. "Sorry." She moved to roll off the bed, but stopped when three heavy knocks sounded from Lillian's front door. Tamara shot her a look. "Who could that be?"

Lillian honestly didn't know. After Joshua dumped her, she'd found a month-to-month lease in Brooklyn. No one knew she was here. And she had no family. Her parents had left her in the foster system when she was six and she highly doubted that they suddenly wanted her back.

She shrugged as she made her way through the living room and pulled open the front door.

A gasp escaped her lips as she stared into the warm eyes and half-smile of Reed Williamson. He was leaning with one arm on the doorframe. He had a sky-blue t-shirt on with acid-washed jeans. His look was both casual and expensive at the same time.

Heat raced to her cheeks when she realized that she hadn't said anything. She swallowed. "What are you doing here?" she asked.

"Is this a bad time?" He straightened and peered past her into her apartment.

"I—uh—I'm packing."

He stepped closer and shot her his intoxicating grin. "Perfect. That's what I'm here for." He hesitated as he glanced back down the hallway. "Well, me and them."

Lillian peered past him to see five men standing in the hallway. They each had on a shirt that said *Hunky Movers*.

"I wanted a shirt, but they said it was for employees only," Reed said.

As his warm breath brushed across her cheek, Lillian realized that he was standing inches away from her. She pulled back to see him staring down at her. Warning bells sounded in her mind as she took a step back. "I've got this handled. Really. There's not much here to even pack. I'm pretty close to being done."

Reed shook his head. "Nonsense. I'm sure we can—"

A squeal sounded behind Lillian, and she winced. Tamara must have discovered who was standing in the hall.

"Are you serious? I mean, you go to the bathroom for one minute and so much happens." Tamara's voice grew louder until she was right next to Lillian.

Reed turned his attention over to Tamara. "Reed

Williamson," he said, extending his hand. He paused. "Don't I know you from somewhere?"

Tamara grasped his hand and shook it vigorously up and down. "I'm one of the nurses for your grandfather. Tamara."

Reed nodded. "Right."

She giggled. "I just have to say, it's mighty nice what you're doing for Lil over here. She's had a crappy last year and you offering her a job like you did..." Tamara's voice cracked, and Lillian took that as a cue to push her from the room.

"I don't think Mr. Williamson wants to hear my life story. Don't you have that thing?" Lillian asked, staring at Tamara, hoping she would get a hint.

"Thing?" Lillian asked.

"Yeah, that work thing you were telling me about."

Tamara stared at her harder before she began to slowly nod. "Right, the thing. I should go and do the work thing." She turned her attention back to Reed. "It was nice to meet you," she said as she stepped past him. "And you"—she lowered her breath as she pulled Lillian with her—"every detail. I expect an invitation to your housewarming party when you're all moved in."

Lillian nodded and then motioned toward the hallway. Thankfully, Reed had already let himself in so there was no way he and Tamara would have to interact when she left.

"I'll be seeing you!" Tamara said as she waved toward Reed and stepped out of Lillian's apartment.

Before Reed could respond, Lillian shut the door.

"Sorry about her," Lillian said as she shot him a sheepish look.

"Well, I only just officially met her, but I kind of like her," he said, smiling over at Lillian.

Lillian leaned against the now shut door. "Yeah, she's great." As her gaze made its way over to Reed, she suddenly realized how alone they were. It didn't seem to bother him one bit. There was a hint of a smile on his lips. Fearing she had something on her face, Lillian reached up and rubbed her nose. "What?" she finally asked, hating how unnerved he made her feel.

He shook his head as he leaned against the back of her couch just as he'd done in his office. "Nothing. I was just wondering if you were going to let the movers in."

She stared at him. And then the memory of the group of men standing in her hallway raced back into her mind. She straightened and pulled open the door. Glancing down the hall, she waved for them to come in.

"So sorry," she said as they piled into her apartment.

They nodded to her as they passed by. Once they were all standing in her living room, she glanced over at Reed who had his hands shoved into his front pockets. He looked so relaxed. How was he this calm?

"Lil, this is Bernard. He'll be packing up your apartment and bringing it to my flat." Reed waved toward the shortest of the five men. He had a bushy beard and was wearing a ball cap. He nodded toward Lillian as he reached out his hand.

"Nice to meet you," Lillian said as she shook it.

"Don't you worry, miss. We'll get you situated and treat your items real nice. My boys are the best in the business. Never broken anything yet."

Lillian's gaze made its way around her apartment. After her divorce, she thrift store shopped. Nothing here really had any sentimental value to her. It had never really felt like a home. Just a holding place while she waited for something more. "You know what? Don't worry about it. Just pack my bedroom and bring all of the rest of the stuff to the Salvation Army."

Reed glanced over at her. "You sure?"

Lillian nodded. After all, she was going to make a killing from this fake marriage. After all was said and done, she'd be able to stock her next apartment with brand new things and not stuff that reminded her of her failed marriage and previous life.

"You heard the lady. This shouldn't take you much time at all." Reed reached out as if to touch her shoulder, but hesitated before letting his hand fall to his side. "We've got other things to do," he said, nodding toward the doorway.

Lillian stared at him. Her heart began to pound as it dawned on her what was really happening. She was going to marry billionaire Reed Williamson. Granted the feelings weren't there, but the paperwork was. Suddenly, she needed a paper bag.

"You okay? You went really white," he said, peering into her eyes.

Lillian swallowed as she forced a nod. "Yeah, I think I'll be okay. I guess I just realized that this was really happening."

An uneasy expression passed over his face. "Is that okay? I know Orson said there's no out, but I'm sure I could come up with something. I could say you died?" He raised his eyebrows.

"That's okay. I really need this," she said. If only Reed knew how true that was.

"You seem to be doing okay."

Lillian stifled a laugh. "Yeah. I'm doing great."

Reed opened the front door and waited for her to pass by him. "Well, after this whole arrangement is over, you'll be sitting pretty."

"That's the goal," Lillian said as she walked out into the hall.

Reed pulled the door closed and then paused to study her. "So we're agreed then."

She shot him a sideways glance. "What?"

"I won't fall in love with you if you promise not to fall in love with me. We'll call this a mutually beneficial arrangement and make sure we both fulfill it without any scars." He leaned closer to her.

She could feel his warmth wash over her. She felt like an idiot when her breath caught in her throat. Of all the times to be stunned speechless, this was not the time. So she found her voice and whispered, "Agreed."

He hesitated before he extended his hand. "Promise?"

She nodded and shook his hand. A tingling sensation started in her palm and raced up her arm. As much as she wanted to pull away, she kept his hand grasped firmly in her own.

"Deal," he said, dropping her hand. He cleared his throat as he glanced down the hall and then back to her. "Let's go get engaged."

CHAPTER FOUR

Reed kept his gaze focused on the road as he drove into the city with Lillian next to him. The silence in his Corvette was deafening. He needed to say something.

Had she felt something as well?

He gripped the steering wheel as he pushed the memories of holding her hand from his mind. There had been a zap of electricity that raced up his skin when they shook hands. It must have been the heat in her apartment. It had felt as if it were one degree from boiling.

He reached over and turned the fan of his blower up a notch. From the corner of his eye, he saw Lillian rub her upper arm. Feeling bad, he turned the air down. "I'm sorry. I'm just really hot. Was your apartment's air out?"

Lillian glanced over at him and shook her head. "That's how it always is. The air conditioning is not the best."

Reed turned his attention back to the road. "You're in for a nice surprise then. I like to keep my flat nice and cool."

He flipped on his blinker and pulled onto the freeway.

After he'd read over the contract that Orson had put together, his mother had come waltzing into the room, proclaiming how relieved she felt now that everything was settled. Reed wanted to shake some sense into her. Just because she forced a girl into contractually marrying him didn't mean that his grandfather was going to sign off on the marriage.

Poor Lillian had to go along with this ridiculous idea even if it didn't end up benefiting him. She was now a part of this messed up arrangement.

He glanced over at her. She was so quiet.

He could tell that there were things about her that she wasn't telling him. Who wants her entire apartment donated? What could have happened that gave her no sense of home?

He wanted her to be able to tell him these things. But she was closed tighter than a ship. And he didn't blame her. For all she knew, he was some crazy guy. Which, after what his mom did, he was beginning to think that perhaps he was.

"You okay?" he asked. He couldn't just let it lie. He wanted her to know that he was here. They were going to be man and wife, after all.

She glanced over at him. There was a confused look in her eyes. Like she didn't know how to answer him. "I think so."

He twisted his hands on the steering wheel. "It'll be over before you know it, and then you can move on with your life."

Lillian snorted.

He shot another glance her direction. What did that mean?

Her cheeks reddened as she leaned back in her chair. "Sorry. It's just you said 'life' like you assumed I have one."

"You have no life?" He rested his wrist on the steering wheel as he relaxed. "Well, I would beg to differ. Your apartment seemed tidy. There wasn't an excess of cats. And you wear jeans, not sweatpants, so you're ahead of most shut-ins."

Lillian laughed. "There you go again. Thinking that hermits and serial killers wear their status on their sleeves. We're sneaky. We only allow people to see what we want them to see."

Reed leaned closer to her. "Should I be worried that you keep referring to yourself as *we*?"

"Yeah, you should be."

He pulled back as he flipped on his blinker and pulled off the freeway. Ten minutes later, he stopped in front of Jezebels and let the car idle.

"What is this place?" Lillian asked, peering out of the window.

"This is where we are going to get clothes," he said as he opened the car door.

When he rounded the hood and handed his keys off to

the valet, Lillian was still sitting in the car. She looked pale. He shot her an encouraging smile and walked over to her door.

"You can do this. It's just shopping," he said as he held out his hand to help her.

Lillian stared at it and then back up to him. "But... This isn't where I normally shop. What does a place like Jezebels sell?"

Reed shrugged. He honestly didn't know. All he'd done was ask his kid sister, Cassie, and she'd told him that this was a trendy store. "Trust me, I have it on very good authority that this is the place to shop."

Cassie had almost blown out his eardrum the night before when he'd called her to tell her about the contract and marriage. She went on and on about finally getting back at Mason for what he did. She said something about fate smiling down on them. Cassie wasn't shy about her dislike for Hannah. Reed appreciated his sister's support, but he was ready to move on and wished Cassie would do the same.

Lillian hesitated, but then set her hand in his. Once she was on the sidewalk, he shut the door and the valet drove his car off. He led her over to the front doors of the shop—reveling in the feeling of her hand clasped in his. Was it bad that he was enjoying it?

They paused as Lillian peeked through the windows. "I'm not so sure. These really don't scream *me*." She waved to the flowing skirts and sleeveless dresses.

"I'm sure you'll look great in whatever you pick out." He

pinched his lips together when he realized what he'd just said. Lillian had heard it too and turned to look at him with her eyes wide. He needed some space from her so he pulled open the door and nodded toward the inside. "Cassie said she'd met you here at twelve-thirty. That's in ten minutes. Go in and look around. I'll text her and tell her you're here."

"Cassie?"

Reed nodded. "My kid sister. She's coming to help you navigate New York's fashion world. She's ecstatic to meet you and make you over." He winced at the phrase Cassie had said. It definitely did not sound natural coming from his lips.

"Really. How does she know about me?"

Reed smiled. "I told her our situation. You can trust Cas. She's amazing. She'll take good care of you."

Lillian glanced up at him. "You're not coming in? You don't need a strapless body suit?" She pointed to the black velvet full body suit that the mannequin had on.

Reed laughed and shook his head. "Not today." As he studied her, a strange feeling brewed in his stomach. Was it wrong that his heart skipped a beat at the possibility that she wanted to spend time with him? He cleared his throat and forced a smile. That was ridiculous. She was just his fake wife. Nothing more. She just didn't want to be stranded in an unknown store.

"I've got a ring to buy." He wiggled his eyebrows. "Big night planned. Mom wants there to be cameras and everything. She wants this to look genuine. So, get a nice dress while you're in there." He waved his hand toward the interior of the store.

Lillian followed his gesture with her eyes and then took a deep breath. "Okay, here I go." She made her way into the store, and Reed let the door shut behind her. She wandered around a few displays, reaching out and brushing her fingers against a few shirts.

Then he remembered her card in his back pocket. Can't have her shopping without money. He pulled open the door and called out her name.

Lillian turned and made her way over to him. "Coming to rescue me?"

Reed shook his head. "Nope. But, I figured you needed money so..." He pulled out the charge card and handed it over.

She took it and turned it around in her hand. "This is mine?" she asked, running her thumb over her name that was embossed with gold on the front.

"All yours. As per the agreement. Unlimited clothing budget. Well, actually there's $50,000 on it. But don't go too crazy and spend it all here." Her skin paled and he noticed she was staring a bit too hard at the numbers across the card. Worried, he ducked down to meet her gaze. Had he said the wrong thing? "Are you okay?"

She pinched her lips together and nodded. "It just feels surreal. I can't believe this is happening." She leaned forward with a twinkle in her eye. "I almost want to get a lottery ticket. I feel strangely lucky."

Relieved that she wasn't upset, a smile twitched on his lips. He liked Lillian. She was modest and humble—two qualities that were sorely lacking in all the women he dated before her. It was nice. "Well, with what you are getting for helping me out, I think we've got you more than covered. Besides, the odds of winning the lottery are about a hundred million to one."

She nodded as she slipped the card into her purse and turned. "Well, I should get some shopping done, and you have a ring to buy." She smiled at him. "I have a very important decision to make between that mohair vest and a pair of suede pants." She wrinkled her nose.

He saluted her and then turned on his heel and headed towards Tiffany's. He slowed his gait the farther he got. For a moment, he contemplated going back into the store to be with her. He enjoyed her company. But he stopped himself before he went too far down that rabbit hole. He was being ridiculous. She was perfectly capable and probably didn't even want him there. She'd just asked to be polite. He pulled out his phone and located Cassie's contact info. He hit the message button.

Lillian is at Jezebels. Where are you?

He hit send and waited.

Five minutes away

He sent a thumbs-up and continued down the sidewalk. Lillian would be fine. Besides, he had a ring he needed to pick out. His mom was adamant that they had to get this right. They needed the whole world to believe that their love was real, or his grandfather would never buy it.

If they blew this, there was no other option. Mason would inherit the company, and Reed would be stuck working for his half-brother and ex-fiancée for the rest of his life.

Muscling down any doubt he had about this arrangement, Reed crossed the street and pulled open the door to the jewelry store. He stepped inside and smiled at the saleswoman behind the counter. She had a tight bun and a pinched expression.

"Good afternoon, sir," she said as she rested her manicured nails on the glass case. "What can I get for you today?"

Reed took a deep breath as he peered down at the rings arranged in neat rows and uttered the words that he never thought he'd say again, "I need to buy an engagement ring."

CHAPTER FIVE

Lillian stood in the shop, glancing around. She had never felt more out of place then she did right now. Wearing her clay-stained t-shirt and jeans had not been the smartest move. But when she'd woken up this morning, packing had been on her agenda. Not shopping at some high-end boutique in New York.

She sighed as she watched Reed slip around the corner and disappear out of sight. There was no going back now. The only person she knew was gone, and she doubted that the valet would let her collect Reed's car so she could high-tail it out of here. The thought of abandoning Reed made her stomach twist, so she pushed all thoughts of running away from her mind. She was stuck in a store that she most definitely didn't belong in—might as well make the best of it.

"May I help you?" a stern voice asked from behind her.

Lillian let out a yelp as she turned to see a severe-looking woman staring at her. She was a good foot taller than Lillian and had a plunging v-neck dress. Her bangs were cut straight across and her nose was long and came to a very defined point at the end.

"I"—Lillian swallowed—"I'm just looking," she said, grabbing a dress off the rack to hold it against her body. She tried to look busy as the woman continued to inspect her.

Just as she pressed the dress to her stomach, the woman let out a disgruntled sound. "Your clothes aren't wet, are they?" She motioned to the stains on Lillian's shirt.

Lillian let out an uncomfortable laugh and hung the dress back up. Of course, this woman singled her out. She no doubt looked like a homeless person who had stumbled in there from off the street. Lillian fought the urge to explain that they were clay stains and not who-knows-what. "No. My clothes have been washed and dried."

The woman quirked an eyebrow. "And you wore them knowing they were damaged?"

Lillian perused absentmindedly through the clothing next to her. "That's how it works for the ninety-nine percent."

The air grew silent. Lillian glanced over at the woman to see that her lips were pinched and her eyebrows drawn together.

Hoping to redeem herself, Lillian forced a smile. "I think I'll be okay for now. I'll let you know if I need to try anything on."

The woman took a step closer to her. "I was actually

thinking that you might find what you're looking for at a shop farther down. At a place—oh I don't know—like Old Navy?"

Lillian stared at her. Was she serious? "I'm..." What was she supposed to say to that?

"Are you Lillian?"

Lillian turned her attention away from the woman in front of her to see a girl with bright blonde hair and a crop top standing a few feet off. She had on a bohemian skirt with chunky sandals that made her look like a Greek goddess.

She raised her eyebrows as if she expected Lillian to say something.

"Am I Lillian? Yes?" she said. Why did she sound so unsure? She'd only been telling everyone her name since she could talk. But the shop attendant had sucked all of her self-confidence out of her. "Are you Cassie?" Lillian leaned toward her.

The girl's ruby red lips parted and she smiled, exposing her perfectly straight, white teeth. "Yes." She glanced over to the shop attendant and narrowed her eyes. "I hope you were treating my future sister-in-law well," she said, reaching out and wrapping her arm around Lillian's shoulders.

The woman's eyes bugged. "I'm so sorry, Ms. Williamson, I had no idea—"

"Save it. We'll be working with someone else." She tipped her head toward the rest of the store and pulled

Lillian with her. "Come on, let's get you away from Trudy. She's the worst."

Relief flooded Lillian's body as she let Cassie drag her to the back of the store. Evening dresses lined the wall. Some had plunging necklines, others dipped low in the back. Right now, all Lillian wanted to do was run down the street to Old Navy. A place where she might actually find something to wear.

"You're so adorable," Cassie said.

Lillian glanced over to see that she'd taken a few steps back and was studying her. Heat rushed to her cheeks. How could an entire group of people unnerve her like this? It was a bit too much. "Thanks," she said, reaching up and tucking a strand of hair behind her ear.

Cassie shot Lillian a smile as she turned and started scanning through the clothing rack next to her. "Now, Reed told me I needed to help you find something fabulous for tonight." She pulled a halter top dress out and glanced down at it.

Lillian wanted to tell her that there was no way she was going to wear that dress, but thankfully, Cassie shook her head and returned it to the rack. She'd put on some weight with this pregnancy and didn't want anything highlighting any of that.

"So, what's your style? Besides stained shirts and jeans?" Cassie asked, casting a sideways glance in her direction before she returned to the dresses.

"Um, that's about it. I try not to buy fancy things

because I always end up with clay stains." She brushed down her shirt. She'd never minded until right now, when she felt like a social pariah.

"Clay? You do pottery?"

Lillian pinched her lips together and nodded. It wasn't something she liked to tell people. Maybe it had to do with the fact that Joshua had never supported her, but she was always nervous about what people would think, so she kept it a secret.

"That's awesome! You'll have to teach me someday," Cassie said as she pulled a floor length evening gown from the rack and held it up to Lillian.

It took Lillian's breath away. The satin fabric felt like butter against her skin as she ran her fingers across it. It was navy and reminded Lillian of the night sky. She grabbed the price tag and almost had a heart attack.

"Five thousand dollars?" she squeaked out.

Cassie shot her a look. "That's not bad. My gala dress last year was north of $10,000." She held it up to Lillian and tipped her head to the side. "This is perfect. Go try it on." She shoved the dress into Lillian's hand and turned back to the rack.

Lillian held the dress as if it were the most expensive item in existence as she made her way over to the dressing rooms and shut the door. She pulled off her shirt and jeans, catching a glimpse of herself in the mirror. Her eyes stopped at her stomach.

Her bump was becoming more pronounced now. She let

her fingers linger on it. Lately, she'd been feeling flutterings in her stomach. As much as she forced herself not to hope, she couldn't help but wonder if it was the baby. Did that mean it was still alive?

After one trip to the doctor to verify the pregnancy, she hadn't brought herself to return. She couldn't get attached to this one. Her heart was still in pieces from the last pregnancy. Going into labor too soon. Not being able to stop it. She squeezed her eyes shut as she pushed the memories from her mind. She couldn't think about that right now. She needed her wits about her.

There was a knock on her dressing room door. "Everything okay?" Cassie asked.

"Yeah," Lillian said, turning away from the mirror and slipping on the dress. She zipped up the back as far as she could and then unlocked the dressing room door.

Cassie's eyes widened. "Wow, that looks amazing on you," she said, twirling her finger for Lillian to spin around.

After the zipper was fully up, she waved for Lillian to follow her to the pedestal in the far corner that was surrounded by mirrors.

Lillian stepped up and glanced at her reflection. The dress was beautiful. It fit her in the top and then flowed around her like a waterfall. How could something so expensive seem meant for her? There was no way she could pay for this.

"I—I need to get this off," she said, stepping down from the pedestal and heading toward the dressing rooms.

"Lillian? Where are you going?" Cassie called from behind her.

As soon as she was inside, she shut the door and locked it. Now safe, she turned and collapsed on the chair next to the mirror.

What was wrong with her? How could she possibly think that this was a good idea? She was going to mess up and fail yet again at something that was important. People never stuck around for her. Reed should just call it off. Take everything she had—which was next to nothing. What did it matter to a billionaire?

"Lillian? Is everything okay?" Cassie's voice was followed by a quiet knock. "If you're worried about what Reed would think, he's going to love it. You look amazing and will totally fit the part he's asked you to play. Don't worry, everyone is going to love you."

Tears filled Lillian's eyes as she took a deep breath. She appreciated how grounded Cassie was. It helped calm her down.

And then she felt stupid. Why was she freaking out? She could do this. She had to. Reaching down, she wrapped her hand around her stomach bulge. Whatever was going to happen with this pregnancy, she needed to be prepared. A single, out-of-work mom didn't seem like the best idea.

So what if she had to fake a relationship? She was sure it wasn't the worst thing someone had done for money. Taking a deep breath, she closed her eyes and counted down from ten. When she reached one, she felt better. Her stomach didn't hurt, and she felt more grounded.

She needed to make the decision right now to marry Reed Williamson. That way, there was no more thinking involved. She would fake this, make the money, and leave. He would get his company, and she'd be taken care of. This was the best option for both of them.

She slipped off the dress and pulled on her shirt and jeans. When she opened the door, she found Cassie on the other side with her eyes wide.

"You okay?" she asked.

Lillian nodded. "Yeah, I'm sorry. I just got overwhelmed."

Cassie clicked her tongue. "I totally get it. I'm sure this is all crazy. When Reed told me what our mom did, I couldn't believe it." She smiled over at Lillian. "But it's a nice thing you're doing for my brother. He deserves this more than Mason. That snake."

Lillian hung up the dress as she listened to Cassie. "Who's Mason?"

Cassie dropped her jaw. "He's our half-brother. The conceived-through-an-affair baby my dad had." She studied herself in the mirror, pushing up her roots as she turned her head to the side.

"What does Mason have to do with any of this?" Lillian sat down on the chair again.

Cassie glanced over at her. "Reed didn't tell you?"

Lillian shook her head.

"Mason stole Hannah, Reed's fiancée, and got her pregnant. Now they're getting married, which means he is fulfilling our grandfather's stipulation to become the CEO while Reed is left with nothing." She gave Lillian a warm smile. "Enter you."

Lillian wasn't sure what to say to that. That seemed like a lot of *personal* information. "Does he..." She studied Cassie. "Do you think he wants me to know this?"

Cassie hesitated for a moment before she shook her head. "I'm sure he'd want you to know. You're marrying him, after all." She reached out and hugged Lillian. "Oh, I'm just so excited that you guys are going to stick it to Mason!"

Lillian patted her back. She liked that Cassie had this open and unabashed way about her. Never had she been so welcomed into any family. Joshua's parents had never approved of her, and she'd been moved from foster home to foster home as a kid. She'd be lying to herself if she said she didn't enjoy this.

"Thanks, Cassie."

Cassie pulled back. "Anytime. Reed's the best brother. He really is the greatest." She raised her eyebrows. "Now, let's blow his socks off with some awesome clothes." She held out her hand and wiggled her fingers. "Hand me the card he gave you and I'll take care of everything. In fact"—she glanced toward the shop's door—"head two doors down to Serenity Salon and ask for Stacy. She'll handle your hair and makeup. Tonight is going to be epic."

Even though the thought to protest raced through her

mind, Lillian nodded and grabbed her purse. What Cassie suggested sound amazing. Just what she needed after the last few days. Plus it helped her get away from this shop with the crazy attendant and prices that made her head swim.

"Thanks, Cas," she said as she stepped out of the dressing room.

"No prob. This is my area of expertise," Cassie said, following after her.

Before she forgot, Lillian pulled out the card Reed had given her and handed it to Cassie. "Just, nothing too wild."

Cassie raised her eyebrows. "I can't promise anything," she said as she took the card.

Lillian turned and headed toward the front door. Once outside, she took a deep breath and glanced down the side-walk. She found the sign for Serenity Salon. When she got to the door, she hesitated then took a deep breath and went inside. It was time to stop worrying about this and jump in with two feet.

She was marrying Reed Williamson, and that was it. There was no going back.

CHAPTER SIX

REED STOOD in his apartment dressed in a suit, staring at Lillian's boxes that had been piled against the far wall. There were only a handful. Apparently, Bernard must have felt that most of Lillian's belongings weren't valuable, because Reed had no idea how an entire apartment could fit in fifteen boxes. He hoped she wouldn't get too upset to see that very little had actually made its way over to his place.

He sighed as he glanced down at his watch. Where were they anyway?

After he'd dropped Lillian off at Jezebels, he went and got the ring, only to get a text from Cassie saying she'd take care of Lillian until their reservations at seven. It was now half-past six and they were nowhere to be found.

The host, Pierre, at The Barbette was not fond of late-comers and was known to give away tables if someone was even a few minutes late. It probably wouldn't happen to him, due to their friendship, but he couldn't be sure.

Groaning, he pulled out his phone and pressed on Cassie's number. Just as he began to text, **where are you**, there was a knock. In three steps, he was at his front door, pulling it open.

He parted his lips to ask his sister where she'd been, but no words came when he saw Lillian's bright blue eyes. Her hair was half pulled up and ringlets framed her face. She had on a dark blue dress that went to the floor. It hugged her curves and wasn't revealing—something most women in his social circle weren't too concerned about.

"Wow," he said. Just as the word left his mouth, heat raced to his cheeks. "I mean, wow, why are you so late?" He turned to see the smug expression of his kid sister.

She had her arms folded as she studied him. "I was taking care of your future wife," she said, blowing past him as she waved her chauffeur into his apartment. "You can bring her clothes to the master bedroom." She waved toward the hall that was to the left of the kitchen.

"Um." Lillian stepped forward. Her eyes were as wide as saucers.

"Guest bedroom, Cas," Reed said, shooting her an exasperated look.

Cassie raised her eyebrows. "Silly me," she said. Then she turned to her chauffeur. "Second door to the right down that hall. She pointed to the hallway just off the main living room.

"I'll go with him," Lillian said as she trailed after the man who was carrying more bags then any human should have to.

Once she was out of earshot, he turned to his sister. "What was that? Geez, way to make her feel weird." Why was Cassie acting so strange? He'd already told her that this was all arranged. There was no actual relationship, emotional or physical, between them.

Cassie shrugged and made her way over to the kitchen, where she grabbed a few grapes from the bowl on the counter. "I like her. You picked a good one," she said, pointing at him.

Was it wrong that his heart picked up speed at the thought that his sister liked Lillian? Yes. It was wrong. He shook his head to clear it and walked over to her. "Yeah, well, you're going to scare her off with all your master bedroom talk."

Cassie shrugged. "Just promise me you won't blow this."

Reed raised his eyebrows. "First of all, I don't blow things, and second of all, she's kind of contractually obligated to stay, so..." He shrugged as he grabbed out a bottle of water from the fridge.

Cassie took it from him before he could even untwist the top. "Well, leave it to you to chase off a woman who is legally bound to marry you." She took a swig and placed the bottle down on the counter. "I need to go. There's a party downtown that isn't going to start without me, and I'm so far behind on getting ready." She gave him a wink and made her way out of the kitchen. "Sawyer, come on!" she said as she pulled open the door. Seconds ticked by before he appeared in the hall.

"Sorry, just helping Ms. Lillian get situated." He made his way out into the hall that led to the elevator with Cassie following behind him.

"Don't mess this up," she sang out as she shut the door.

Thankful that she was no longer there to embarrass him, Reed took a deep breath. Before he could gather his wits about him, Lillian appeared. She looked unsure as she glanced around. Her eyes were wide. Compared to her apartment, his flat had to feel huge with thirty-foot ceilings and giant picture windows.

His mother had insisted he hire her decorator, who had a flare for the modern. Half his furniture was either white or black. Most times, he felt as if he lived in a black and white movie. It was decorated well, but it never really felt like his.

"Everything okay?" he asked, shoving his hands in his pockets. He wasn't sure what to do and felt exposed standing there.

Lillian's gaze fell to him. "It's like this is a dream," she said.

"You dream in black and white?"

She drew her eyebrows together. "What?"

"Never mind," he said as he opened the fridge and grabbed out a water bottle. Then he eyed her, suddenly feeling like he needed a reason to approach her. "Here," he said, extending the beverage.

Lillian glanced down at it. "Thanks," she said as she took it and unscrewed the top.

He tried not to stare at her, but she was truly breathtaking. There was nothing fake about her. She was genuine, and he was drawn to that.

"What time is dinner?" she asked, glancing over at the clock.

He shook his head. How could he have forgotten? "Seven. We need to go," he said, extending his hand toward the front door. Out of instinct, he pressed his other hand on her lower back. He felt her muscles tighten, and he instantly regretted it. But before he removed his hand, she relaxed.

There was an inner tug inside of him. One part wanted him to keep as far away from Lillian as he could. The other part wanted to keep touching her. It felt right in a way he couldn't describe.

Thankfully, there was no need to touch during the fifteen-minute drive to Barbette. When they pulled into the valet parking, Reed cursed under his breath. He'd forgotten to tell Lillian about the cameras. He hoped they wouldn't scare her off.

Lillian glanced over. "Is everything okay?"

Reed shook his head. There were a few photographers standing at the front door. They were glancing around as if hoping for the next big story.

"It's just that my mom actually called a few local magazines to let them know that we would be here." He waved toward the cameras.

Lillian's eyes widened. "Why would she do that?"

He shrugged. "Evidence, I'm assuming." He glanced over at Lillian, who looked as if she was going to be sick. "We can go someplace else." He knew that this was a lot to ask of someone.

Lillian clutched her purse as she stared at her lap. Then she shook her head. "Let's do this," she said, turning and giving him a confident look.

"You sure?"

She nodded. "Let's give them something to write about."

He smiled at her as his fingers found the door handle and pulled. He stepped out of the car and handed his keys to the attendant who approached him. As he made his way over to the passenger door, flashes started going off around him.

"Who are you here with tonight?" a photographer asked as he raised his camera and took some shots.

"You know I don't give out names," Reed said as he pulled on the door handle and extended his hand to Lillian. She grasped it and allowed him to help her out.

She squinted as the flashes picked up speed. Once her door was shut, she moved closer. Hoping it was okay, Reed wrapped his arm around her waist and pulled her to him. They smiled at the cameras and allowed a few more shots.

"Come on," Reed said, leaning down to whisper in his

ear. "They won't follow us into the restaurant. Pierre wouldn't allow it."

Lillian nodded. The movement caused her perfume to waft up around him. He fought the urge to breathe it in.

When they were moments from the front door, a photographer called out, "What? No kiss?"

Lillian tensed as Reed turned around and shot them a smile. "You think I'd make it that easy for you? Come on, and they say you're good at your job."

There was a chorus of laughter as Reed opened the door and ushered Lillian inside. Flashes were dulled when the front door shut behind them. Pierre was standing next to the host's desk. He was a short man with black hair that glistened in the overhead lights. His gaze met Reed's and he smiled. They'd been friends for a long time. This was one of Reed's favorite restaurants. It was a bit like home here.

"Good evening, Mr. Williamson. I see the paparazzi have followed you again. They tried to come in and use the bathroom, but I ushered them out." He quirked an eyebrow.

Even though it seemed as if Pierre was joking, Reed knew that he liked to keep his high-end clients anonymous. Mobs of photographers at the front door did not sit well with him. Leave it to his mother to offend Pierre. "I know. I'm sorry. My mom insisted that this dinner be publicized." He shot Pierre a smile, hoping it would make up for the cameras.

Pierre attempted to narrow his eyes in a serious manner. "Just don't let it happen again." He laughed, his expression changing to welcoming host as he waved his hand toward them. "Your table is ready for you," he said.

Reed nodded and motioned for Lillian to follow him. She kept in step as Pierre led them into the kitchen and over to the chef's table. Clanging of dishes and people talking in Italian filled the air. When Reed glanced over at Lillian, her eyes were wide.

"We're eating in here?" she asked.

Reed paused. "Is that okay? It's my normal table."

Lillian glanced over at him and then nodded. "Yes," she breathed out. "I've just never sat at a table like this before. I see it all the time on cooking shows and always wondered what it would be like..."

He watched her as Pierre motioned for her to slide into the half-circle booth that lined the far wall. She was so amazed by the smallest things. He liked that she didn't know anything about his world. It was refreshing to see his life through a new set of eyes.

"You may sit," Pierre said, extending his hand.

Reed clapped him on the shoulder and nodded. "Thanks for doing this," he said and then slid in next to Lillian.

Pierre gave him an exasperated look before he flipped the wine glasses over. He was always telling Reed to stop thanking him for just doing his job. "What will we be drinking tonight?" he asked.

Reed glanced over at Lillian.

"Water is fine."

"Madam, we serve the best wines in the country. Perhaps you would like to see the list?" He reached into his suit coat pocket.

Before he could pull it out, Lillian shook her head. "No alcohol for me, thank you."

Reed studied her. Lillian kept her gaze on the white table cloth in front of her.

"And you, Mr. Williamson? Scotch on the rocks as normal?"

Reed shook his head. "Actually, I'll have a water."

Lillian glanced over at him and he shot her a smile. "Don't feel like you can't drink on my account," she said.

Reed shrugged as Pierre walked away. "It's okay. I probably drink a bit too much as it is."

Lillian smoothed out the table cloth as she glanced around. "It's beautiful in here. Makes my dingy apartment kitchen look like a dump."

Reed leaned back, relaxing his legs. One brushed against Lillian. For a moment, he hesitated, wondering what she would do. She shifted but didn't pull away. His heart hammered in his chest. What was wrong with him? He was acting like a teenage boy. But he wasn't going to move. He liked the feeling of Lillian next to him.

"So, besides your love of kitchen architecture, what else should I know about you?" He unbuttoned his suit coat, which helped him feel more relaxed.

"Me?" Lillian pointed her finger toward her chest.

"Nothing really. I'm pretty boring." Her cheeks hinted pink as she fiddled with the silverware.

Reed liked how nervous she was. "Okay. Well, if we are going to pull this fake marriage thing off, I'm going to need to learn something about you."

She chewed her bottom lip. Reed couldn't help but notice how soft and full they looked. When she glanced over at him and he realized that he was staring at her mouth, he snapped his gaze up to meet hers.

"Well, I love art."

Reed clapped his hands as he leaned forward, hoping to distract himself. "That's something. Is it painting? Drawing?"

"Clay. I love pottery."

Reed nodded. Truth be told, he didn't know too much about that. His mother dragged him to all the galleries in Europe, but nothing really held his attention. "Do you just like studying it or do you do it?"

Pierre returned with some sparkling water and poured them each a glass. He announced that the chef was whipping up something new and exclusive just for them and then left.

Now alone, Lillian peered over at him. "I do both. Study and create."

"You'll have to show me sometime." A waitress brought them a basket of bread and they each grabbed a piece and began eating.

It was nice, sitting in silence next to Lillian. She had a

calming effect on him. Even though they'd just met, he was grateful to have her by his side. And for some reason, he wanted to learn more about her. An excited feeling brewed in his gut. Perhaps, this whole arrangement wasn't going to be terrible after all.

CHAPTER SEVEN

Lillian couldn't believe the tastes and sensations that she was experiencing here at the Barbette. This was hands down the best meal she'd ever had. It wasn't until her stomach felt as if it was going to burst, that she laid her fork down and leaned back.

Reed was studying her as he wiped his lips on his napkin. There was a twinkle in his eye. "Did you like the meal?"

She couldn't help the satisfied smile that formed on her lips. "It was amazing. Do you eat like this all the time?"

Reed set his napkin down on the table and nodded. "Yeah. Perks of the lifestyle, I guess."

"I'm going to be the size of a house by the time our contract is over," she said.

Reed shot her a quizzical look before he nodded. "Contract. Right." He patted his suit coat.

The waitress stopped at their table to clear their plates. Reed shifted in his seat as he glanced over to her. His leg brushed hers again, sending tingles across her skin. Heat permeated her cheeks as she kept her leg there, pressed against his. Was it wrong that she was enjoying it?

"So, when we head back out there, I'm going to propose to you. Mom wants the press to document it. Thinks it will help convince my grandfather." He patted his chest again. Lillian could only assume that he was making sure the ring was still there.

Lillian took a deep breath. Once he proposed publicly, there was no going back. She was going to become Mrs. Reed Williamson. Her heart quickened at the thought. But then she pushed it from her mind. There was no way she was supposed to be excited about that.

The money? Yes.

But not the title. The marriage was just an advantageous one. It didn't mean she was wanted. And it didn't mean that she was family. Desperate to distract herself, Lillian laughed and said, "Tamara's going to freak."

Reed took a sip of water. "What are you going to tell her?"

Lillian shrugged. Tamara would be suspicious, sure, but Lillian was sure the shock would fade once the realization of what the marriage meant settled in. "I'm sure once I get talking about the wedding plans, she'll be just fine."

Reed tapped the tabletop with his fingers. "About the

wedding. I was kind of hoping we could keep it small. Just my mom and my sister along with my grandfather. We could have a priest perform it in my grandfather's room. You could invite a few people if you want." He raised his eyebrows. "Your family?"

Lillian pinched her lips shut and shook her head. "Foster kid. The only family I have is Tamara. Well, there was Joshua, but—" She cleared her throat as she stared down at her hands. What was wrong with her? Bringing up her ex's name? That was a road she didn't want to go down. The less Reed knew about her past the better.

When she glanced over at him, Reed had straightened and was studying her. "Who's Joshua?"

She waved his question away. "An old relationship turned sour."

A knowing look passed over Reed's face. "I understand that."

Lillian wanted to ask him if he meant the girl now engaged to his half-brother, but kept quiet instead. She really didn't want him to know that Cassie had spilled his history to her. Plus, it was strange, but she kind of wanted Reed to trust her enough to tell her himself.

He clapped his hands and rubbed them together like he was preparing to do something sinister. "Are you ready for this, Ms. Brunette?"

Lillian nodded. "Ready as I'll ever be."

"You do realize that once we do this, the press will start digging into your closet." He leaned in and raised his eyebrows. Geez, he smelled good. "There aren't any skeletons that I should know about, right?"

Panic rose up in her chest. She had secrets. A very big, yet very tiny secret. But she couldn't tell Reed. She couldn't tell anyone. This pregnancy wasn't going to last, and she couldn't get her hopes up. So she forced a smile and shook her head. "No skeletons."

Reed swiped his forehead. "Whew."

After thanking the chef, Reed pressed his hand on her lower back and led her from the kitchen. At first, his touch had made her shy away, but she was slowly becoming accustomed to it. It comforted her in a way that both excited and scared her. The desire to be cared for also came over her, and she let the contact remain.

Pierre waved at them as they passed by, heading out the front door. The paparazzi were idling around on the sidewalk, trying to look busy.

Reed cleared his throat, and their gazes whipped over to them. "You guys are still here," he said, wrapping his arm around Lillian's waist and pulling her close.

Lillian's heart hammered so hard in her chest that she feared it would give her away. Could he hear it? Could the photographers?

Reed seemed so calm and collected. Why was she the only one having a reaction from his close proximity? She needed to get a grip. This was fake. It wasn't real. A dream that could be taken away from her at any moment. Besides, she had promised herself and Reed that she wouldn't have feelings for him, and she was going to keep her word.

"Are you going to give us anything we can use?" a short photographer with a fedora asked.

Reed hesitated before he turned and grabbed both of Lillian's hands. He met her gaze and gave her a wink. Even though she knew what was about to happen, her breath caught in her throat as she watched him lower to one knee. That got the attention of all the photographers and they began snapping photos. Their flashes blinded Lillian.

"Lillian Brunette, I knew the moment you walked into my office that you were going to change my life." He met her gaze and gave her his half-smile. Despite her better judgement, her insides melted a bit. "I can't imagine my life without you by my side. I want you there, walking with me through the good times and the bad." He let one of her hands fall as he released it to reach into his suit coat. He removed a ring. The diamond was so big it dazzled as it caught the remaining light from the setting sun.

There was a low murmur of appreciation from the crowd around them. Lillian couldn't help but stare at the ring. Never in her life had she imagined she'd get to wear something that beautiful. The one Joshua gave her was from the discount store. She almost feared what would happen when Reed turned it over to her.

"Will you, Lillian Brunette, agree to marry me and make me the happiest man in the world?" He lifted her left hand and readied the ring on her fourth finger.

Fear crept up inside of her, but she pushed it away. She needed to say yes, no matter how scared it made her. She was contractually obligated to marry Reed. End of story.

"Well?" a nearby photographer asked.

Right. She was supposed to answer. She glanced down at Reed who was looking up at her expectantly. "Yes," she said as excitement bubbled up in her stomach. Reaching out with her right hand, she cradled his cheek. "Yes, Reed Williamson. I will marry you."

He glanced down and slid the ring on her finger. Then he stood, wrapping her into a hug. For reasons she couldn't describe, it felt right. They fit together. She wrapped her arms around him as he brought her closer, pressing her body against his. They held each other for a moment before he pulled away.

They turned to the photographers and smiled.

A woman with a bob did not look impressed. "Seriously? No kiss?" She rolled her eyes as she glanced at another photographer who shook his head.

"You gotta kiss. That's what the people want to see," fedora interjected.

"You want a kiss?" Reed glanced around and received a unanimous nod. "They want a kiss, sweetheart."

Lillian started to protest but then swallowed. She needed to make this real. "Then let's give them a kiss." She turned toward him.

The look on Reed's face almost made her laugh. Suddenly, his cool and collected persona was shaken. His eyes were wide as he peered down at her. "Are you sure?" he whispered.

Lillian smiled and nodded.

Reed slid a hand around her waist and pulled her close. She could feel his muscles under her hands as she rested them on his chest. He leaned in closer, until he was inches from her. His presence intoxicated her, making her knees weaken and her head spin.

Thankfully, he was holding onto her. If not, she feared she'd slip from his grasp and collapse on the ground.

"You can back out if you want," he said, as he leaned in closer, taunting her with his lips.

She narrowed her eyes. "Absolutely not. I'm going to earn that money."

He backed away slightly with his eyes wide.

Great. That didn't sound right. "You know what I mean," she said, leaning in and hoping he'd follow.

"I'm a little scared to find out," he said.

"Just kiss me so they have a picture." She tilted her face toward him.

He hovered for a moment and then pressed his lips against hers. Heat raced from her lips, across her skin, and exploded throughout her body. Her heart hammered so hard, she thought it might leap from her chest and take off. What was happening to her? This kind of a reaction from a kiss?

She wanted to pull away. Break this connection she felt with Reed Williamson, but she couldn't. Every part of her begged to get closer to this man standing in front of her.

He deepened the kiss, pulling her so close that she feared she wasn't ever going to be the same. But, despite her better judgment, she slid her hands up his chest and to the back of his neck. She entwined her fingers together and pressed him closer to her.

Hoots and whistles could be heard around them as lights flashed against her eyelids. The reality of what she was doing came rushing back to her. She was kissing her not-really-in-love-with-her fiancé. Sure, they were getting married and she was finally getting the family she'd wanted since she was a kid. But it didn't mean that it was real.

At least not to Reed.

In an act of self-preservation, Lillian released her hold on him and stepped back. Her lips felt swollen as she glanced up to see Reed peering down at her. His eyebrows were drawn together and his gaze hazy. Had he felt the same thing too? Or was he just trying to figure out why she'd kissed him like that.

"That was..." he whispered.

Lillian wasn't sure what he was going to say, so she turned toward the cameras and shot them a smile. Talking to the photographers seemed like a better idea then listening to Reed dissect what their kiss meant. Either conclusion scared her.

"What's your name?" a reporter called out.

"Lillian Brunette," she said. Her chest tightened. She

hoped that she wasn't going to regret telling them who she was. But it was her job to fake this relationship, and they were going to find out anyway.

"How long have you been dating the billionaire bachelor?" the woman with the bob asked.

Lillian stood there, with her lips parted. They hadn't gone over any of that. What was she supposed to say? A day?

Suddenly, Reed appeared next to her. He wrapped his hand around hers. His warmth comforted her. "I've got this sweetie," he said as he leaned closer to her. "My fiancée and I are leaving to spend the evening celebrating our engagement. You won't fault us for not answering your questions." He raised her hand and kissed it. "After all, we can't make it too easy for you."

The valet appeared and handed Reed his keys. Lillian let him lead her over to his car, where he pulled open the passenger door and helped her in. Then he jogged around the front and got into the driver's side. When his door was shut, he shifted the car into drive and pulled away.

Once they were driving, Lillian relaxed into her seat. She glanced over to Reed, who was studying the road. His wrist was perched on the top of the steering wheel, and he seemed so relaxed. As if they hadn't just experienced a mind-bending kiss.

She folded her arms and focused outside. Why was she being so ridiculous about this? It must be her pregnancy hormones that were out of control. They were making her feel and think things that weren't real.

"Are you okay?" Reed's voice broke the silence.

Lillian pinched her lips together and nodded. "Just tired. I'm ready for bed."

Reed smiled over at her. "I'll get you home as soon as possible."

Home.

Lillian returned her gaze back outside. She wasn't sure what Reed's place was, but she knew it wasn't home, no matter how much she wanted it to be.

CHAPTER EIGHT

Reed drove the rest of the way back to his flat in silence. He was thankful that it gave him time to think and digest exactly what had happened to him.

Lillian's kiss had caught him off guard. It felt right and real. Something he hadn't experienced in a very long time. And that scared him. How could he have a reaction like that for his fake wife? He was beginning to realize that coming out of this relationship unscathed might not be possible if he didn't get his head on straight and focus.

He pulled up to the door of his building and put his car in park. Harold, his door man, hurried over. Reed smiled over at Lillian, who was moving to pull on the door handle.

"Harold will get that for you," Reed said, nodding toward Harold who was standing just outside her door.

Lillian glanced over and hesitated. Harold pulled it open and extended his hand.

"Good evening," he said, smiling down at her. Harold was a short, balding man. He insisted on wearing a full suit in the middle of summer which made his head glisten with sweat.

Lillian nodded to him and took his hand, allowing him to help her out. Reed shut his door and rounded the hood of his car. He handed the keys over to Harold, who nodded.

"Have a good evening?" he asked.

Reed glanced over at Lillian. "Got engaged."

A pink hue tinted Lillian's cheeks as he saw her twist the ring with her thumb.

Harold's eyes widened. "Wow, boss. That's amazing. Congrats."

Warmth rose up from his stomach. Why did the thought of being with Lillian make him feel this way? It was ridiculous. Perhaps because marriage had been on his mind for so long, but felt so far away, the fact that it was really happening was messing with his head.

Harold climbed into the driver's side and pulled away. Turning, Reed smiled over at Lillian who was watching him. "Ready?"

She nodded and followed him as he made his way through the lobby and into the elevator. He punched in the code that took him to his flat. That was probably something he needed to tell her.

"My code is 1771. For when you want to go places."

Lillian glanced over at him. "Thanks."

The doors closed, leaving them alone in the elevator.

The gears hummed to life and began carrying them up to the twentieth floor. Reed was racking his brain for something to talk about. But what does one say to a person whose kiss just kind of, sort of, knocked his socks off? Polite conversation didn't seem like enough.

"Have you lived here long?" she asked.

Grateful that Lillian had been the first to break the silence, Reed smiled over at her. "Since Hannah—" he pinched his lips together. As soon as her name came spilling out of his lips, he knew that a conversation about his past was the last thing he wanted to have on the evening of his engagement. She should be the furthest thing from his mind. And Lillian didn't need to know his history. "For about five months."

When he turned his attention over to her, Reed noticed that Lillian was studying him. As if she suspected what he was going to say. And maybe she knew. The magazine articles weren't too kind about the situation. But Lillian didn't seem like the kind of person who would read the gossip columns, so Reed decided to assume that she knew nothing. It was less painful that way.

Thankfully, the elevator chimed, and the doors opened to the small hallway that led to his door. He walked across the plush carpet and pulled out his key. "I'll have Harold make you a copy," he said as he unlocked the door and stepped into his flat.

Once Lillian was inside, Reed shut the door and hung his key on the wall. He made his way into the kitchen, where he grabbed out two bottles of water and offered her one.

"I know how much you love water," he said, giving her a wink.

She was standing close to the door as if she felt like she didn't belong. That was the last thing Reed wanted. This was going to be her home as well—or at least that was what the contract stipulated. She might as well feel comfortable.

"You okay?" he asked as he wiggled the bottle in her direction.

Lillian smiled and took the water. She studied him for a moment, parting her lips as if she wanted to say something. Then she shook her head and untwisted the cap. "You've got quite a decorator," she said, glancing around his living room.

Reed followed her gaze. He wasn't sure he would classify his flat like that. "My mom's decorator came in and did this." He waved his hand around. "Not really my taste, but what can you do?" He took another swig of water.

Lillian wrinkled her nose. "Yeah. It's a little too black and white for a home. A dentist's office, maybe. It needs some color."

"Feel free to add anything to the decor. I want you to feel like you belong here."

There was a shift to the intensity of her gaze. Almost as if she didn't know how to process what he'd said. Then she swallowed and raised her eyebrows. "Are you sure?"

"Yep. This is going to be your home too. I want you comfortable. Besides, I'm rarely here anyway."

Her eyes widened as she glanced over at him. "Really? So, I'm going to be here alone?"

Maybe his mom really didn't think this through. From the expression on Lillian's face, being his wife was not the profession she wanted. He gave her a quick smile. "You can do anything you want." An idea popped into his head. "In fact, I have an office right next to the guest room you're staying in. Why don't you turn that into your own office?"

She dropped her jaw. "I couldn't do that. It's your office."

He shrugged. "You are going to be my wife. I want you happy." He thought for a moment. "Don't they say, happy wife, happy life?"

She tapped her water bottle with her finger. "Yeah. They do say that."

"I aim to please," he said, waving his hand toward his chest.

Lillian began to nod her head more enthusiastically now. "Okay. I can get on board with that."

Reed reached out and brushed her arms with his fingertips. What started out as a comforting gesture quickly had his skin tingling and his heart pounding. But, there was no going back now, so he kept them there for a second longer before he dropped his arms and shoved his hands into his front pockets.

Lillian glanced over at him. There was something in her gaze that hinted to him that she might have felt something, too. Before he drove himself crazy trying to decipher her expressions, he smiled. Saying something seemed like the best distraction. "Just no fluffy pink pillows or pictures of babies dressed as vegetables."

She raised her eyebrows and forced a shocked expression. "But that's the only thing I decorate with."

"I knew it. I knew it when I looked at you that you were that kind of decorator."

She laughed. A soulful, genuine laugh. It was the first real laugh he'd heard from her, and he liked it. Once it died down, a wave of exhaustion passed over her face. "I should get to bed. I've got a big day of unpacking tomorrow." She nodded toward the small stack of boxes.

"Yeah. It's been a long day." He glanced in the direction of the guest room. "Can I walk you to your place?"

She hesitated but then nodded. "Sure."

They walked next to each other the one hundred feet from the kitchen to the guest bedroom. She paused and nodded toward the door. "This is me."

He reached past her to get the door, bringing his chest inches from hers. He could smell her perfume, and the feeling of her body so close to his almost paralyzed him. When he turned the knob and pulled back, he glanced down at her. She was right in front of him. It would be so easy to lean down and kiss her again. Was it wrong that he wanted to?

She gave him a small smile and ducked her head. "Thanks for walking me to my place."

Reed chuckled as he watched her walk into the room.

He leaned one arm against the doorframe, not wanting to leave her presence. When she turned, she met his gaze.

A sudden need to say something washed over him. "Thanks for doing this."

Lillian scoffed and motioned to the room. "I should be thanking you. This is the best place I've ever lived in." She pinched her lips together as her cheeks turned red.

"Well, you're doing me a huge favor." He pushed off the door and gave an exaggerated bow. "So I owe you."

Lillian laughed again. "Any time."

Reed grabbed the door handle and began to close the door. "Have a good night, Lillian."

"You too."

Just before the door was shut, Lillian said his name. Reed hesitated, wondering if he'd heard right. His mind was swimming from everything that had happened tonight. It was possible he'd imagined her speaking.

"Reed?" her voice was low as she appeared in the slit of the door.

He pushed open the door. "Yes?"

"Do you mind helping me with my zipper?" She turned slightly and motioned toward the back of her dress.

His heart hammered in his chest as his eyes widened. Had she really asked him for that? Before she changed her mind, he nodded. "Sure," he said. His voice had come out lower than he'd intended.

Get a grip, Williamson.

Lillian turned so her whole back was to him. He

couldn't help but stare at how creamy her pale skin on her neck and arms looked. He reached out and grasped onto the top of her dress, letting his fingers linger against her skin. A fire ignited in his stomach.

She tensed and tilted her face toward him. Reed cleared his throat as he focused on the task at hand. It was as if everything was moving in slow motion. He grabbed the zipper and slid it down. He saw the lace from her undergarments, and forced himself to step back. This was not where he was supposed to be. He needed to leave.

"There," he said, moving out into the hall.

Lillian turned, holding the front of her dress against her body. "Thanks," she whispered. Her gaze held his for a moment.

He gave her a smile, nodded, and pulled the door closed.

Now alone, Reed leaned against the wall and blew out a breath. What was happening to him? He scoffed as he pushed off and headed to his room. He was losing his mind; that's what was happening. Somehow, this woman had turned him into a babbling idiot.

Scrubbing his face with his hand, he closed his bedroom door. He needed to get a grip. All of this was fake. She was leaving as soon as he became CEO, and if he didn't get a hold of himself, he was going to end up hurt. That was something he'd promised himself he would never do again. Only an idiot would allow feelings for a woman who was contracted to be with him.

And he wasn't an idiot.

THE NEXT MORNING, Reed's phone buzzed next to his bed, waking him up.

He groaned and slapped his nightstand, trying to find the offender. Once he found it, he hit the talk button and flipped onto his back. "Yeah?" he asked, draping his elbow over his eyes.

"Mr. Williamson?"

"Uh-huh."

"It's Persephanie. Johnson wanted me to ask you if you'll head to Dallas today to speak to Motor Designs. Apparently, they are considering pulling out of the deal."

Reed pulled his arm from his eyes and glanced over at his phone. "He can't handle it?"

"They want you. Won't talk to anyone else."

He clenched his jaw and pulled off his covers. "Got it. I'm up. Tell Drew to ready the plane. I'll be there in an hour."

"Yes, Mr. Williamson."

He grabbed his phone as he headed across his room to the door. He needed coffee before a shower. When he got to the kitchen, he started his machine. As it whirred to life, he leaned against the counter and yawned.

"Oh, I'm sorry." Lillian's soft voice startled him.

He turned to see her standing on the outskirts of the kitchen. She was wearing a baby blue night shirt, and her hair was pulled back in a loose braid. His heart raced from how beautiful she looked with the early morning light peeking in through his windows.

"You're up early," he said.

Her gaze kept flicking down to his chest, and he became very aware that he was standing there without a shirt. It amused him that her cheeks had turned pink. He made sure to fold his arms, hoping it caused his muscles to flex.

She dropped her gaze, tucked an escaping curl behind her ear, and stepped into the kitchen. "I needed to use the bathroom and heard some noise."

Reed tried to keep from staring at her long, creamy legs as they came into view. When he saw her bare feet, he smiled. He liked that she felt comfortable enough to be casual around him.

"Ah. Just me." He cleared his throat and turned, grabbing down two mugs from the cupboard behind him. "Sleep well?"

"Despite the need to pee every hour, yes," she breathed out. He glanced behind him and saw a content look cross her face.

And then she swallowed and her cheeks reddened as if she suddenly realized what she'd said. "You didn't need to know how many times I went to the bathroom."

He shrugged. "Hey, I like it that you feel comfortable enough to tell me everything."

She let out a nervous chuckle. "Your mattress is amazing. I haven't slept on a bed that comfortable in"—she glanced up toward the ceiling—"in ever. I've never slept on something that comfortable."

He smiled as he turned his attention back to the coffee, which he poured into the mugs. "I'm happy you liked it." He handed her one.

She wrapped her fingers around the handle and studied it. Then she sighed and placed it next to her. "I'm on a sort of coffee fast," she said.

Reed raised his eyebrows as he took sip. The warm liquid ran down his throat, heating his stomach. "I have heard coffee addiction is a real killer in the modern world," he said as he lowered his mug.

She gave him a small smile. "Well, one can't be too careful."

Reed studied her. What was her story? "So, no alcohol or coffee, huh?"

She pursed her lips and nodded. "Yeah, I'm boring that way."

"It's intriguing." His phone chimed, so he put his coffee down and pulled it from his pocket. Persephanie had sent his itinerary. And he was already running behind.

He turned back to Lillian. "I'm leaving town for a few days on business. I have to go to Dallas to talk an investment off the ledge." He paused as he glanced down at her, and her eyes widened. "I'll be back soon. Until then, make yourself at home. Desiree, my housekeeper, she's quite a character. She'll be here at eight. Let her know if you need anything. Do you still have that card I gave you?"

She nodded.

"I'll put more money on it. Go and get what you need to make this place comfortable for you." He leaned closer to her. He wasn't sure what the protocol was for a long absence from a woman he was supposed to pretend to love. Did he hug her? Kiss her goodbye? Instead of making a decision, he gave her a one-armed hug and pulled away. Embarrassment coursed through him, heating his entire body. Why was he such a bumbling fool sometimes?

Deciding it was best to leave before he did another idiotic thing, he started toward his room then stopped. His mom was most likely not going to be happy that he was leaving town. She had made it very clear that they were to be married immediately. But, she was going to have to wait. There was nothing to inherit if the company went under.

"My mom will most likely want us to wed when I get back. Call Cassie and ask her to take you shopping." He ripped off a piece of paper from a nearby pad and wrote down Cassie's number. "I'm sure she'll love to take you out again."

He walked over and pushed the scrap into Lillian's hand, trying to ignore the surge in his chest from their contact. He glanced down at her and she met his gaze. Truth was, he didn't want to leave. But distance from his contract wife was probably smart. The feelings brewing in his gut were confusing him.

"Stay safe. I'll be back before you know it."

Lillian nodded. "You too." Then she tilted her head. "I mean, stay safe."

He leaned down and brushed a kiss on her cheek. Then he turned and left the kitchen before he saw her response. Once he got into his room, he walked straight into his bathroom and started his shower. He needed to get out of here. He was enjoying this fake relationship situation a bit too much.

CHAPTER NINE

The early morning sun crept into Lillian's room, waking her up. She stretched out on the bed as she stared up at the ceiling. Her body ached from all the shopping Cassie had made her do yesterday. From the moment Reed left until nine o'clock at night, it was nothing but store after store, trying on this and that.

It was exhausting but in a good way. While trailing behind an enthusiastic Cassie, Lillian began to wonder if this was what it was like to have a sister. And she hadn't realized how much she longed for it. Tamara was great, but her job forced her to be gone for weeks on end. With no one else in her life, Lillian was used to being alone.

But being around Reed and the people in his circle, she found herself enjoying all the company. It made her realize how much she wanted a family and a place to belong.

A flutter raced across Lillian's stomach, grounding her in

the present. She reached down and rested her hand on her stomach. Realization of what that meant settled in around her. She was nearing month six. That meant, if she went into premature labor, there was a chance that the baby could survive.

Survive.

The word echoed around in her mind and caused her heart to pick up speed. For a moment, she allowed herself to hope. But she pushed that ridiculous notion out of her head and pulled her covers off. She was made to be alone. Hoping for a life outside of what she was destined for was ridiculous. It was time for her to stop wishing and get moving.

Boxes of unopened decorations were scattered throughout her room. She hadn't had any time to hang anything up. As soon as she got back from shopping, she had gone straight to bed.

She climbed out of bed and shuffled over to her door, where she paused. She could hear faint singing. Who was here?

Twisting the door handle, she peered out of her room toward the kitchen. The light was on and someone was opening and closing cupboards all the while singing a song in a language Lillian didn't recognize.

"Hello?" she called out, making her way toward the intruder.

The noise stopped and suddenly, a woman with dark, curly hair appeared. "You must be Ms. Lillian," she said, crossing the space between them and wrapping her into a hug. After a few uncomfortable seconds in the arms of this stranger, the woman pulled back and kissed both of Lillian's cheeks. "I am Desiree. I came yesterday but you weren't here." She waved Lillian toward the kitchen.

Lillian hesitated, but followed. "I'm sorry. I was out with Cassie, shopping."

Desiree laughed. It was deep and throaty. "That sounds like Ms. Cassie. She's always shopping." Desiree motioned toward the table where a plate was sitting. "Sit. I made you breakfast," she said.

Lillian complied and took a seat. Desiree appeared and dished her up a portion of a quiche.

"I hope you like eggs."

Lillian nodded. "That works."

She ate while Desiree whirled around the kitchen, putting dishes away and mopping the floor. It seemed strange that this woman was already cleaning an impeccably kept house, but what did she know? The wealthy lived very differently than she did.

"How long have you known Reed?" Lillian asked as she took another bite.

Desiree paused and began tapping her fingers. "Well, it was about a year before he met Hannah, so..." She glanced toward the ceiling. "Seven years."

Lillian swallowed sharply and a piecc of crust scraped her throat. She coughed as the pain of the bite radiated in her chest.

Desiree looked concerned, but Lillian just waved her away.

Once her coughing fit was done, she took a sip of the water that Desiree had placed in front of her. "They were together that long?"

Desiree had returned to mopping. "Yes. They'd known each other since high school. That's why what she did to Mr. Reed was just awful." She spat on the ground but then mopped it up.

Huh. "He must have really loved her," Lillian said, taking another bite.

Desiree nodded in time with the rhythm of the mop. As silence fell around them, Desiree glanced over at Lillian. A sheepish expression passed over her face. "I mean, he did. But he's moved on." She gave Lillian a wide smile. "With you!"

Before Lillian could respond, there was a knock. Desiree motioned for her to remain seated as she made her way over to the door. There were some muffled voices and then Desiree nodded and shifted to the side.

"Office is the first door on the left," she said, waving toward the hall off of the kitchen.

Three burly men stepped in, nodding in acknowledgment. They passed by Lillian, each mumbling a hello and then disappeared down the hall.

"What's going on?" Lillian asked as she stood and made her way over to the sink. Desiree appeared next to her, taking her dish before she could set it down.

"Mr. Reed has a surprise for you," Desiree said as she wiggled her eyebrows.

Lillian's heart quickened. "A surprise? For me?" She let out her breath slowly. There was no need to get her hopes up. She was lying to herself if she said that she didn't miss him. Thankfully, Cassie had kept her distracted yesterday. "Have you spoken to him?" Lillian asked, glancing sideways at Desiree.

"Yes. We spoke. He is flying in tonight." She studied Lillian. "It's lonely around here without him, huh?"

Lillian cleared her throat as she dropped Desiree's gaze. She didn't want Desiree to see her reaction to the news. Her stomached lightened to hear that Reed was on his way back. Then dread filled her chest. She still had boxes to unpack and an apartment to decorate and deep down, she wanted to surprise him with having it all done.

"What's the matter?" Desiree asked.

Lillian steeled her nerves as she tried to shoot Desiree a confident smile. "I was hoping to surprise Reed with a few of my decor touches, but I'm not sure I can do it all."

Desiree dropped the rag she was using to wipe off the counter and turned. "Honey, you are speaking my language. Let's do it."

DUSK SPILLED in through the windows as Lillian pulled the roast she'd been cooking out of the oven. The smell of carrots and potatoes filled the air. She placed the dish on the stovetop and turned, yelping as she pressed her hand to her heart.

The oldest of the three men who had been working on the office, was standing behind her with his hat in his hands. Lillian had been too busy with Desiree to notice what the men were doing all day, and had completely forgotten they were even there.

"Yes?" she asked, clearing her throat.

"I just wanted to let you know that my men and I are finished and will be getting out of your hair."

Lillian nodded. "Well, thank you."

He smiled and waved toward the two men behind him, who straightened. They all nodded and said "Ma'am" as they passed by.

Now, alone, Lillian glanced toward the hall. What had those men been doing back there? Just as she took a step toward the room, she heard the lock on the front door turn. Her heart picked up speed as she brushed down the apron she'd bought and tucked a loose strand of hair behind her ear.

The door opened, and Reed walked in. He paused as he glanced into the kitchen. His eyes widened. Lillian took this moment to study him. He looked worn out. The top buttons on his shirt were undone, and his tie hung around his neck.

Feeling awkward standing there, staring, Lillian took a step toward him. "You're back," she said.

Reed turned and a smile spread across his lips. "Wow,"

he said, leaving his suitcase by the door and glancing around. "You did all of this?"

He was being too kind. A few pictures and couch pillows. Little splashes of color here and there. Nothing mind-altering. "It wasn't that much," she said, feeling sheepish about how much she wanted him to like what she'd done.

He glanced over at her, giving her an approving look. "Well, it looks a lot less like a show room and more like a home." He shrugged out of his suit coat and hung it on the back of the chair. "Did you cook?" he asked, walking over to the stove and dipping down to smell the roast.

"Yes," she whispered. What had felt like an exciting surprise now seemed like a stupid mistake. What had she been thinking? Reed wasn't her fiancé. He wasn't hers to take care of. This was a contractual marriage. It had an expiration date. Besides, what was he going to do when he found out she'd withheld a huge secret? She wasn't going to be able to hide this pregnancy much longer.

A sour feeling rose up from her stomach. She was such a fool. She'd allowed the excitement of a potential home and a person to care for her take over.

"It really wasn't a big deal. I was just bored."

Reed turned and studied her with his eyebrows furrowed. "You've been bored? I thought Cassie was going to take you out."

Lillian stepped forward with her hand raised. She hadn't meant to offend Reed, just push off the feelings that were lingering in her chest. "She did. It was nice. I guess, I was just lonely here."

He glanced around. "I understand. This isn't your home."

"Or life," she whispered. Heat raced to her cheeks. Why had she said that out loud? The look on Reed's face was hard to read. For a moment, she thought she saw a flicker of hurt in his expression.

"I understand that," he said, grabbing his suitcase and wheeling it behind him. "I'm going to unpack and take a quick shower. Then I can join you for dinner." He passed by her without glancing over.

Lillian nodded, her chest squeezing from the sudden distance he put between them. She didn't mean to hurt him. She just wanted to guard herself. Reed was too nice. If she wanted to walk away from this contract unscathed, she needed to build a wall.

Fifteen minutes later, Reed emerged from his room in a t-shirt and pajama bottoms. His hair was damp, and he looked refreshed. He shot her a smile as he made his way over to the table where she sat and pulled up a chair.

They ate in silence. When Reed was finished, he set his silverware down and glanced over at her.

She gave him a smile, hoping to make up for earlier. "I'm sorry for what I said."

Reed studied her. "It's okay." He leaned forward, not breaking her gaze. "I get it. This was probably not how you dreamed of meeting and marrying a guy. And after this, what, you're going to tell people that you're a divorcee?"

Lillian tried to ignore the ache that took up residence in her chest. If he only knew how true that statement already was. There was nothing about the past few years that came even close to what she'd dreamed of. She leaned forward, hoping she seemed more relaxed than she felt. "And you? Was a contract a part of your dream when it came to love?"

He laughed and stacked his utensils on his plate as he stood. "Oh yeah. I always imagined that my mother would be involved as well." He winked as he made his way over to put his dishes in the sink.

"Typical of a teenage boy," Lillian said as she grabbed her dish and joined him.

He hesitated, pressing his hands down on the counter. When she neared, he glanced over at her with a serious expression. She wondered what he was thinking. Did she want to know?

She turned on the faucet and rinsed her dish. Reed turned and leaned against the counter with his arms folded. Suddenly, the memory of him standing shirtless in the kitchen that first morning raced back to her. Her cheeks heated as she tried to force the image of his muscular chest from her mind.

"Truth is, I always thought I'd have the normal guy-meets-girl kind of romance. Fall in love and have boatloads of kids."

Lillian paused and glanced over at him. A sadness crept

up inside of her. That was definitely not their relationship. At all.

"But this is better. No feelings, just a mutual agreement." He tipped his head, cracking his neck. "It's literally written in the contract that we can't get hurt. All relationships should be like this."

Lillian nodded as she focused on the plate she was rinsing. Why did it hurt to hear him say those things? It was the truth. After all, that's what they'd agreed to in the beginning. "Agreed," she said, forcing a smile.

He studied her and then turned his attention to the windows. "Did Patrick stop by?" He squinted over at Lillian. "He's my contractor."

"Patrick. That was his name? There were three guys working in your office all day."

"Did you go in there?"

Lillian glanced over at him. "Was I supposed to?"

He shook his head as excitement brewed in his gaze. "Come with me," he said, waving toward her.

"Right now? I'm doing the dishes."

He turned off the water then reached down and grabbed her hand. Her heart stuttered as he entwined his fingers with hers and motioned for her to follow him.

Lillian took a deep breath and forced her feet to move. When they stopped outside the office door, Reed glanced over at her. She couldn't help but notice that he kept her hand wrapped in his. Did he enjoy it as much as she did?

"Are you ready?" he asked.

"I'm not sure. Should I be worried? We covered me not being a serial killer, but I never asked you." She hoped humor would hide the nerves that raced around in her stomach. What could he have possibly done?

But instead of denying it, Reed just laughed and rested his hand on the door handle. "Close your eyes."

Lillian gave him an exasperated look and then complied. She waited, straining to listen as the click of the door handle filled the silence. He guided her into the room and turned on the light.

"Open your eyes," he said.

Lillian hesitated and then peeked through her eyelids. When she saw a pottery wheel, her heart picked up speed. Glancing around, her lips parted. His entire office had been turned into a pottery studio. There was a small kiln in one corner, with paints and a clay roller in the other. Lillian stepped farther into the room, turning to look at Reed.

He looked sheepish as he glanced over at her. "Do you like it?"

Lillian had no words. When Reed began to look concerned by her silence, she nodded. "It's beautiful. Is it for me?"

Reed laughed as he walked over and ran his fingers over a nearby shelf. "Well, you don't want to see what kind of pottery I would do."

Before she could talk herself out of it, she crossed the floor and wrapped her arms around him. As much as she wanted to keep her distance, no man had ever treated her as kindly as Reed Williamson had. A hug felt appropriate for what he'd done.

He hesitated at first but then returned the hug. She closed her eyes as she memorized how it felt to be held by him, because in a moment she was going to need to pull away.

"Wow," he said, his voice low.

"Thank you," Lillian replied before she dropped her arms and fled the room. Once she was in the safety of her bedroom, she shut the door and collapsed on her bed.

Why did Reed have to do that? Everything about this arrangement had just become that much more complicated. She was getting in too deep and this was not going to end well, no matter how much she might want it to.

CHAPTER TEN

The next morning, Reed called Persephanie and canceled all his appointments. There was one very pressing meeting he needed to attend to, and he wasn't looking forward to it. He needed to introduce Lillian to his grandfather—as his future wife.

Reed swallowed as he stared up at the ceiling. Why was he so nervous about this? All his grandfather had said was that he needed to be married to inherit the company. There was nothing in his stipulation that said Reed had to love the woman.

Love.

His heart picked up speed when he thought about Lillian. It was a feeling he hadn't allowed himself to think he could ever feel again. Not since Hannah. But, somehow, Lillian was beginning to wiggle her way into his mind, confusing even his most ingrained decisions.

Feeling ridiculous for even thinking about having feelings for his fake fiancée, Reed threw off the covers and climbed out of bed. He needed a shower and some clean clothes.

Fifteen minutes later, he was dressed. Pulling open his bedroom door, he walked down the hall to find Desiree in the kitchen. She was dancing and lip-syncing while wiping the counter tops down. She stopped when she saw him approach.

"Good morning, Mr. Reed. I didn't wake you, did I?" she asked as she pulled out her ear buds. A worried expression settled on her countenance.

Reed shook his head. "No. I was up." He walked over and grabbed a banana from the bowl on the counter. "Either I slept in or you're here early," he said, taking a big bite.

Desiree waved away his comment. "No, I'm early. It's my nephew's birthday today and I have to be in Long Island for his party." Her expression grew soft as if she were lost in a memory.

Reed finished the banana and threw away the peel. "That's awesome. I hope you have fun."

She stopped wiping the counter and studied him. "What's with you? You're acting different." She raised her finger and wiggled it in his direction.

Reed shook his head. "I don't know what you are talking about."

Desiree narrowed her eyes and then blew away the strand of hair that had come loose from her bun. "It was the dinner, no? I told Ms. Lillian that the way to a man's heart is through his stomach." She raised her eyebrows and shot him a smile. "They should call me the love doctor."

Reed folded his arms as he leaned back against the counter top. "Love doctor? Really?" That was the last thing he needed—Desiree thinking it was her duty to insert herself into his love life.

"You never know. It could be my calling," she said, shrugging.

"This is a fake relationship," Reed said and then stopped himself. He turned to see Desiree's eyes widen. Crap. He'd forgotten that she didn't know. "But you can keep that a secret, right?"

Desiree chucked a towel his direction. "Mr. Reed, I clean your house. Trust me, I can keep a secret."

Reed started to laugh, but then stopped. What did that mean? Before he could ask, Lillian came walking into the kitchen. Her eyes were heavy with sleep. Her hair was tousled, and she had on a t-shirt and shorts.

"Oh, Ms. Lillian. We didn't wake you, did we?" Desiree turned around and swatted Reed with the towel she'd retrieved. "You woke up this poor woman."

Reed raised his hands. "Hey, now. If anything, it was your singing that startled her awake." He reached up and wiggled his finger in his ear as if the noise was too loud.

Desiree looked unimpressed. "I have a wonderful singing voice," she said, gathering her cleaning supplies and taking off toward his room. "I'm going to start in here. I hope there aren't any *secrets* that I might have to keep."

Reed parted his lips and stepped toward her, but Desiree ignored him as she slipped into his room. Knowing she was just joking, Reed chuckled and turned his attention back to Lillian. She had her arms folded across her chest.

"Can I get you a drink?" Reed asked, suddenly feeling the need to do something. After last night, he wasn't sure what to say to her. He knew he'd upset her, but he still wasn't sure why.

Her cheeks hinted pink as she nodded and sat down on a bar stool. "Thanks. Water."

Reed nodded. "Coming right up." He walked over to the fridge and pulled it open. After grabbing a bottle of water, he set it on the counter, nudging the fridge door closed with his hip.

After he started a pot of coffee, he glanced over at Lillian. She looked contemplative as she studied him. Should he bring up the previous night? He wasn't sure if she wanted to talk about it.

"Thanks for what you did. That studio is amazing. There are professionals I know that don't have a state-of-the-art studio like that." She fiddled with the water bottle cap.

Reed's chest swelled. She liked it. Even though her reaction last night had left him worried, her words put him at ease. He hadn't screwed up. He nodded. "I'm happy you like it. It's all yours. I want you to feel like this place is your home." He glanced around, taking note of the splashes of personality she'd put up around his apartment. It looked less sterile and more like a home.

"That's kind of you," she said.

There was a moment of silence while Reed met her gaze. For the first time, he held it. He allowed his feelings to brew in his stomach. There was a connection here that was growing harder for him to deny. The intensity was getting strong—he needed to break away.

"Eggs," he blurted out.

Lillian raised her eyebrows.

Heat raced across Reed's skin. He could be such an idiot sometimes. "Sorry. Would you like me to make you some eggs?"

"Oh. Sure."

Reed nodded, grateful for the task. He busied himself in the kitchen, grabbing the eggs from the fridge and a pan. Once oil was heated, he cracked the shells and watched as the yolks and whites sizzled in the pan.

"Toast?"

She nodded.

Reed sliced some French bread that Desiree always bought him from a bakery down the street. He slipped the slices into the toaster and then turned. With nothing to do, he shoved his hands into his front pockets and studied Lillian.

"Wow, this is amazing. You could run a bed and breakfast," she said. He reveled in the hint of a smile that played on her lips.

"I could, couldn't I?" He grinned at her. Was it wrong that he liked the fact that she saw him as a capable person? Most women he dated whined that he didn't have a full time cook to wait on their every whim. It was refreshing that he could feed his guest himself without complaints. That Lillian appreciated that he wanted to do something for her.

Once their food was served, he grabbed both plates and nodded toward the table.

Lillian followed him. Once she'd taken her seat, Reed handed her a fork, and they ate in silence.

When they were finished, Reed grabbed her plate and stacked it on his. Lillian thanked him and leaned back.

"Did you have any plans for today?" Reed asked. He wasn't sure how she was going to react to him wanting her to meet his grandfather. But it needed to happen. Might as well pull that Band-Aid off.

Lillian's gaze made its way over to him. "No. Not particularly."

Reed nodded. "Good. I want to visit my grandfather and introduce you to him. That way, when we announce that we are getting married soon, it won't come as a shock. My grandfather doesn't really read the tabloids, so he probably hasn't heard."

Lillian's eyes widened. "What? You want me to meet him? Now?" She shifted in her seat.

"Yeah. Is that okay? I mean, you're going to have to meet him soon anyway." He shot her a supportive grin. "Plus, this way, it can be just you and me."

Her cheeks reddened as she glanced up at him. "I guess," she said. Her voice was quiet as she dropped her gaze to study the tabletop in front of her.

Relief washed over Reed. Having her agree lifted the weight that had been sitting on his shoulders. If his grandfather didn't believe that they were for real, then this whole situation was for nothing.

"Give me a half hour to shower and get ready," she said, pushing away from the table and standing.

Reed nodded and watched as she walked out of the room. He breathed out the air he'd been holding in, and studied the plates in front of him. He could do this. It was just one meeting.

Desperate for a job to do, he brought the dishes to the sink. Just as he picked up the dish wand to wash them, Desiree appeared, grabbing it from him.

"What are you doing, Mr. Reed?" she asked, peering into the sink.

"Washing a plate."

She tsked and bumped him with her hip. "I don't think so. I'd be out of a job if you learned how to do what I do." She motioned for him to leave. "I'll take over. You go relax or do push-ups. Or whatever it is that you wealthy types do."

Reed parted his lips to protest, but she shot him a no-nonsense look, so he backed off. As he walked out of the kitchen, he realized that he had twenty-five minutes of idle time. This was not good. His mind was racing with thoughts of Lillian; he needed a distraction.

After ten minutes of aimlessly wandering around his flat, Reed finally settled down on the living room couch, next to one of Lillian's additions. A fluffy red pillow that tickled his arm every time he moved.

He tried to get comfortable, but the cushions on the couch had very little give to them. Probably because no one had sat on it since it'd been brought here six months ago. When he'd left the home that he and Hannah were going to share, because he found out she'd cheated on him.

Clearing his throat, he leaned forward and grabbed a book off the coffee table in front of him. It was titled, *Botched Taxidermy.* Flipping it open, he glanced down at a picture of a fox whose eyeballs had been put in wrong. Instead of staring straight ahead, one was looking up while the other looked down.

As he flipped through the book, the more ridiculous the mistakes became. He couldn't help but laugh at the frog that had been dressed up to look like Kermit. When it got to the strange concoctions of animal parts, he shut the book. Those just might give him nightmares.

He set the book down on his coffee table and looked around. He was going to have to ask Lillian if he should be concerned that she'd decided to bring it into his house as decoration.

Movement by the hallway caught his attention. He turned to see Lillian entering the living room, wearing a full-length dress. It was white and embroidered with blue swirls. It had a beach feel to it when she walked. Her hair was pulled back into a bun at the nape of her neck. She looked like a Greek goddess.

Suddenly, he had the desire to call Tristan, his pilot, and whisk her away on his jet to Greece, where they'd lounge on the beach and watch the sun set over the ocean. But that might overwhelm her, so instead, he stood and did a sort-of half bow.

Feeling stupid that he couldn't get his thoughts in order, he laughed off his response. "Sorry. Don't know where that came from."

She quirked an eyebrow. "Yeah."

Desperate to move away from the strange feelings brewing in his chest, he steepled his fingers and brought them to his lips. Then he pointed toward the book he'd been thumbing through. "Botched Taxidermy?"

Her cheeks reddened as she approached. "Sorry about that. I think the shopkeeper was playing a joke on me. She told me that all the high-end socialites were buying it." She rubbed her temple. "In hindsight, she might have been teasing me."

He laughed as he approached her. "It's okay." He reached out and hovered his fingers inches from her arm. "I would have probably listened as well."

Her gaze dropped to his hand, and she glanced up at him. "I thought I would enjoy shopping, but being there just proved to me how out of place I feel in stores like that."

Reed studied her. "What happened?" Was there something she wasn't telling him?

She held his gaze for a moment before she dropped it. "Never mind." She turned and headed toward the door. "Ready to go?"

He followed after her. "Lillian, what happened?"

She shook her head. "It doesn't matter. It's in the past."

Reaching out, he grabbed her elbow to stop her retreat. "Why won't you tell me? Did someone treat you badly?"

She kept her gaze trained on his chest. Then she took a deep breath. "It started at Jezebels and continued at all the stores Cassie took me to. Everyone could see I wasn't rich and treated me as such."

Anger built up in his chest. "What? Who?" He grabbed his phone. There was no way his fiancée was going to be treated this way.

Lillian reached out and wrapped her fingers around the phone. "It's okay. I'm sure it's pretty normal. I don't look like a billionaire. I'm a nobody. I would have tried to kick me out if I were them."

He stared at her. How could she possibly believe what she had just said to him? She wasn't a nobody. She was rapidly becoming a very big somebody to him. He reached out and placed his fingers under her chin and slowly raised her face until she was looking straight at him.

"You are not a nobody. I don't ever want you to say that about yourself again." He met her gaze with as much intensity as he could muster without scaring her. "If that ever happens again, tell me. I will be down there as fast as I can to deal with the situation. You are going to be my wife, and nobody does that to my family."

Her eyes widened as she stared at him. Then she blinked a few times. "Thanks," she said.

Reed dropped his hand and nodded. "Now, let's stop talking about this or I just might have to go down to those shops and give them a piece of my mind."

Lillian reached over and grabbed her purse. Once it was strung over her shoulder, she followed him out the door. Reed watched her press the elevator button. Anger roared in his stomach, but he tried to tamp it down. There was no need to get all hot-headed. She assured him that she was okay. He was just finding it hard to believe her.

All he knew was if anyone attempted that when he was around, they would have a world of hurt on their hands. Nobody treated his future wife like that. Even if she wasn't really his, he'd protect her, no matter what.

CHAPTER ELEVEN

All it took was a thirty-minute boat ride to Reed's grandfather's secluded island to make her forget everything that had taken place in Reed's apartment. It must have been the light blue skies and the salty breeze that helped take her mind off of how protective Reed had gotten when he'd found out how she had been treated. Or that he had called her his family.

She swallowed as she rubbed her upper arms. Even though it was warm, the wind whipped around her, chilling her skin.

"Here," Reed's low voice said from behind her.

She turned to see that he'd removed his suit coat and was holding it out for her.

"Thanks," she said, slipping in one arm and then the other.

He helped her pull it up onto her back. For a moment,

his hands lingered on her shoulders before he dropped them. Her skin tingled from the absence of his touch.

Swallowing, she glanced over at him. "This is amazing."

Reed squinted toward the water that surrounded them. "Yeah. Grandpa Williamson knows how to pick a place to call home."

Lillian nodded. "He really does."

The boat captain, Roger, pulled the boat up to the dock and left it idling. Once it was secured, he opened the gate and rolled out the walkway that led from the boat to the dock.

Lillian could feel Reed hesitate next to her. It was as if he didn't want to leave. Feeling the urge to comfort him, she reached out and entwined her fingers with his. She felt his gaze bore into her as he studied her. Not sure what to do, she started to walk toward the dock.

Reed followed her, keeping contact. Her heart hammered in her chest as she stepped onto the dock, still holding his hand. It was almost like they belonged together. Like they were meant to do this all along. Her mind swam with thoughts of Reed. How he'd taken care of her. Let her into his life that already had so many people in it. What a contrast to her lonely one.

They made their way across the backyard and up to the house that sat at the top of the hill. The outside walls were completely covered with grey stone. The same material made up the steps and patio that led up to huge windows and two open sliding doors. Drapes waved and shifted in the breeze.

There were pots, exploding with flowers, next to tall lampposts that hugged the path they were on. Lillian couldn't help but sigh from the utter beauty around her.

Reed's soft chuckle drew her attention. He was watching her, which was surprising. How could he be looking at her when there was so much to see around them?

"Do you like this place?" he asked. His voice grew louder as he leaned toward her.

He was inches away. She could feel his closeness even though only their hands were touching.

Lillian focused her thoughts and nodded. "It's beautiful."

"It is."

When she glanced up at him, she saw him staring down at her. A rush of emotions raced down her spine and throughout her body.

Warning bells sounded in her mind. This couldn't be happening. There was no way Reed had feelings for her. She couldn't get through this arranged marriage if the guy she was supposed to be faking a relationship with developed feelings for her.

Even though her heart ached to stay, Lillian dropped Reed's hands and stepped away from him. She folded her arms, only to realize that she was still wearing his suit coat. She slipped out of it and handed it over.

"Thanks for that," she said.

He studied her with his brows knit before he reached out and took it. "No problem." He narrowed his gaze as if he were trying to figure her out. "You can still wear it if you need it."

She shook her head. "I'm okay." Then she cleared her throat, trying to dispel the lingering feeling of Reed's hand against her own. "We should probably get our story straight before we go in there and your grandfather sees right through our act." She shot him a smile that hopefully came across as confident.

Reed glanced toward the house. "Okay. How about we met, fell in love, and got engaged?"

She tapped her chin as she stepped away from him. "Yeah, probably need to be more specific." She turned abruptly and hesitated. Reed had moved to stand right behind her. Her heart raced, so she moved away from him. "Let's say that we met four months ago at a party. Afterward, I went to Europe to study art and we kept in contact—"

"And then I slowly fell in love with you so when I found out I needed to marry, I knew you were the girl for me. I raced across the ocean to get you and bring you back." There was a hunger to his gaze that scared and excited her.

She broke his gaze. None of this was real. She'd never studied anything in Europe and Reed had never suddenly decided he loved her and raced to win her over. The relationship wasn't real and neither were any feelings they might have for each other.

"Perfect. It explains my absence and your sudden engagement." Feeling satisfied with their story, Lillian climbed the stairs to the house.

She didn't pay attention to whether Reed followed her. Right now, the more distance she put between them, the better. When she got to the back door, she hesitated. Reed appeared next to her and reached out, grabbing the handle.

He pushed open the door and extended his hand for Lillian to follow. After Reed introduced her to a woman named Clarissa, who was his grandfather's assistant, he led her up a grand staircase in the middle of the house and down a hall lined with doors. She watched as he paused just outside the last door. A look of unease spread across his face.

He was nervous. Why was he nervous? Should she be nervous, too?

Deciding not to dwell on the unknown, Lillian met his gaze and gave him a smile. "It'll be okay. I can pull this off. You'll be single and CEO of Williamson Investments before you know it."

His gaze lingered on hers. He nodded and opened the door.

A clicking sound filled the silence as she followed Reed into the room. A giant, four-poster bed sat in the center of the room. Machines with blinking lights surrounded the bed. Lillian's gaze fell on a thin man who was lying on top of a mound of pillows. His grey hair was combed over, and his skin was thin and pale.

He opened his eyes, and when his gaze landed on Reed, he smiled.

"Reed, you came to visit me," he said.

Reed swallowed and nodded, approaching the bed.

Not sure what to do, Lillian hung back, keeping to the shadows.

As if he suddenly realized that she was no longer next to him, Reed scanned the room. When his gaze fell on her, he motioned for her to come closer.

She shook her head for a moment, but when she saw the pleading in his gaze, she moved until she was standing a few feet away. Reed reached over, grabbed her hand, and brought her closer.

"Who did you bring with you?" his grandfather asked. His tired gaze swept over Lillian and then back to Reed.

"Grandpa, this is Lillian Brunette." He lifted her left hand and showed the ring on her fourth finger. "We're engaged."

Mr. Williamson's eyebrows rose as he studied Reed. "Engaged? I didn't know you were dating anyone."

Reed nodded and told his grandfather the exact story that they had perfected outside. Mr. Williamson listened, but his expression never changed. Did he believe it? Would they actually be able to pull this off?

After Reed finished, Mr. Williamson turned his attention over to Lillian. "Reed, leave us."

Lillian's heart picked up speed as she involuntarily held tighter to his hand. There was no way she wanted to be left alone. What if she said something stupid and ruined Reed's chances? This was way too much pressure to put on her.

"I—um, is it okay?" Reed glanced down at her. She could see his internal struggle.

Holding her breath, Lillian calmed her nerves and nodded. "Of course."

Reed gave her hand one more squeeze and made his way out the door, which he shut behind him.

Now alone, Lillian suddenly realized how large this bedroom was. Solid oak floors with matching trim made the room seem dark and intimidating. She hugged her chest as she turned to see Mr. Williamson studying her.

"So, Lillian, my grandson says you've been dating for a few months?"

Lillian swallowed and nodded. "Yes," she squeaked out. She cleared her throat and tried again. "That's right. We met, and then I went to Europe." Ugh, why did her answers seem so robotic? What was wrong with her? She needed to get a grip, or she was going to tip off Reed's grandfather.

"What part?"

Lillian's mind felt muddled. "Excuse me?"

Mr. Williamson shifted on the bed, pushing himself up higher. "What part of Europe were you staying in?"

Suddenly, her entire mind went blank. How does one forget every country in a continent? "Oh, you know. All the major cities. It was an art museum crawl, so to speak. You know, like a pub crawl." She wanted to smack her forehead. Who says that?

Mr. Williamson studied her and slowly began to smile. "I like you."

Her eyes widened. "What?"

"I like you. You're not like the girls that Reed used to bring around. You're different, and that's refreshing." He smoothed the blanket that was draped over his lap. Then he brought his gaze back up to Lillian. "You will still need to get married. I can't make any changes to that. If Reed doesn't, he will lose the company to Mason."

Lillian nodded. If only his grandfather knew that she was contractually bound to marry him, he probably wouldn't have said that. But the more she was getting to know Reed, the more it felt like an opportunity instead of an obligation.

His grandfather sighed and leaned back on the pillows. "Once it becomes legal, I'll sign the company over to him."

Relief flooded Lillian's body. She hadn't screwed anything up. Reed was going to get exactly what he wanted, and that made her happy. Then the thought of what that meant for her poked its way into her mind. Once Reed got the company, would he still want anything to do with her?

She mentally slapped herself. What was wrong with her? Of course not. He wasn't going to want to stay married. She wasn't his wife, and he wasn't her husband. And they most certainly didn't love each other.

When she glanced back over at Mr. Williamson, she saw that his eyes were closed. Not wanting to disturb him anymore, she tiptoed from the room. She shut the door quietly behind her and turned, yelping when she saw Reed standing inches from her.

His eyebrows rose expectantly. "So?"

She let out the breath she'd been holding and took a step back. She needed to calm her mind and her racing heart. There was an expiration date to their relationship. She needed to remember that. He wasn't here for the long haul. As soon as he got what he wanted, he was going to leave her. Just like everyone else in her life. Just like the baby inside of her would.

But she couldn't say anything. The last thing she wanted was for Reed to stick around because he felt guilty. So she forced a smile. "He approves. As soon as we get married, he'll sign the company over to you, and we are through."

Reed's lips spread into a wide grin, and before she could stop him, he wrapped her up into a hug, pulling her off the ground and spinning her around.

When he set her down, he kept her close as he glanced down at her. Her heart hammered in her chest. Why was he this close? Didn't he know how confused he made her feel?

He hesitated before he dropped his lips closer to hers. Was he going to kiss her again? Her mind screamed at her to back away. But her heart begged for him to lean down, tell her he wanted her to stay forever, and kiss her.

Her heart sank when he brushed his lips against her cheek and whispered, "You're amazing. Thank you." Then he pulled back and clapped his hands as he blew out a breath. "Best news ever," he said, grinning at her.

She nodded, forcing her confusing feelings down into the pit of her stomach. "Of course. It's in the contract. Get you the CEO spot so we can move on with our lives." She forced a smile, even though her words tasted bitter on her tongue.

Reed hesitated as his expression grew serious. A look passed over his face and he parted his lips.

Lillian wasn't sure she wanted to know what he was going to say. She didn't need him to tell her that she was a great girl and, as soon as she became single, she'd have her pick of men. She didn't need him to assure her that the perfect guy was still out there. Right now, she needed some fresh air.

"I'm feeling a bit nauseous. I'm going to go outside." She turned and started down the stairs.

When she got to the bottom, she breathed a sigh of relief. Reed had not followed her, and she was grateful for that. Right now, she needed a break from all of this. She needed a moment to collect her thoughts and stifle her feelings. If not, by the time this was all over, she was going to find herself alone with a broken heart, and she wasn't sure she could survive that again.

CHAPTER TWELVE

THE NEXT MORNING WAS SATURDAY. Reed stretched out on his bed, staring up at the ceiling. The early morning light was peeking through the slits in his drapes. He rubbed his face and glanced over at his clock.

Seven thirty.

After their intimate conversation at his grandfather's house, they'd kept the topics light until they needed to leave. On the boat, Lillian had spent most of the time with her arms wrapped around her chest, staring out at the ocean. When they got to his apartment, she had said she was tired and slipped into her room.

Reed had watched her retreat before he made his way to his room, where he dove head first into work. He hadn't been able to fall asleep until midnight. As much as he wanted to say that it wasn't because of Lillian, he knew that would be a lie. It very much had to do with how confused he felt about her.

Now awake, he groaned and sat up. This was not what he should be dwelling on. Right now, he needed to focus on marrying her, and that was it. Leave all thoughts about feelings at the door.

He pulled off his covers and stood. Then he made his way over to his bathroom and flipped the shower on. Fifteen minutes later, he emerged with a towel wrapped around his waist. He walked over to his phone, only to find that he had twenty missed calls from his mom.

Which didn't surprise him. He swiped his phone on and played one of the many voice messages.

"Reed, it's your mother. I heard you went and visited your grandfather. He seems in good spirits, so I thought we might as well get this wedding over with."

Reed snorted as he got dressed. Just like his mother to feel like the wedding equated to seeing the dentist. It was something to check off the list.

"Get Lillian and meet us at your grandfather's estate this evening at five. Everything will be taken care of. We just need you to show up." The phone grew silent, indicating that the message was over.

Reed reached over and played the next message.

"Reed. Where are you? Why aren't you answering? Call me as soon as you get this so I know you are coming. I don't need to remind you how important it is make sure this wedding happens. I would hate to hear what your grandfather would do if Mason decided to up his wedding. Thank goodness, Hannah is in Milan sorting out a clothing debacle this week. I've been so stressed trying to juggle all of this." She sighed. "I'm ready to get this over with."

Reed buttoned up his shirt as he rolled his eyes. His mother always had a *the sky is falling* mentality. He rolled the cuffs of his sleeves and grabbed his phone.

Three rings, and his mother answered.

"Where have you been?"

"Well, good morning to you, too." He pressed the phone to his ear as he turned the door handle and headed out into the hall.

"Reed, I am not amused. I've been running around since five this morning, trying to make sure this wedding is going to be perfect. The least you could do is answer my phone calls."

"Mom, calm down. I was in the shower. I figured you didn't want me calling you while I was in there."

There was an exasperated sigh on the other end of the call. "I'm not in the mood for this. Please just tell me that you and Lillian will be at your grandfather's estate tonight."

Reed walked into the kitchen, where he grabbed an apple out of the bowl. "We'll be there."

"Thank you."

"Love you." Reed said.

"Love you, too."

Reed hung up the phone and set it down on the counter. He turned and pulled open the fridge to grab a jug of milk.

Soft music carried from down the hall. After Reed poured a glass of milk, he replaced the container and followed the music.

He paused just outside of his old office and listened. A whirring sound contrasted against the classical music. A smile played on his lips. Lillian was using the studio.

Reaching down, he turned the handle and pushed open the door. Lillian's back was to him. Her hair was pulled up into a messy bun at the top of her head. Her elbows were brought up and rose and lowered in a smooth movement. She was humming along with the music.

Reed's gaze fell to the cut off shorts she had on, accentuating her long, slender legs. As his gaze made its way up, he saw that the collar of the oversized t-shirt she wore slipped off her shoulder every time she brought her arms down. His heart pounded in his chest when he remembered how smooth her skin had been under his fingertips.

He shook his head and stepped into the room. "You seem to be enjoying this," he said.

Lillian yelped and let go of the tall vase she was working on. It bent and began flopping around as the wheel continued to spin. She grasped her heart as she whipped her gaze over to him. "You scared me," she whispered as she took calming breaths.

Reed raised his hands. "Sorry. Didn't mean to distract you."

She pushed some of her hair away from her face with the back of her hand. Despite her best efforts, she wiped a streak of clay across her cheek. The wheel stopped spinning as she stood. "Did I wake you?" she asked as she scraped the clump of clay off the wheel, brought it over to a bucket, and dropped it inside.

"No," he said as he leaned against the wall and watched her.

She glanced over at him. "I should have known. You look more prepared for the day than I do." She waved toward her clothes.

"How long have you been at this?"

She squinted as she placed the lid on the bucket. "Since six." She wiped her hands on her shorts and smiled over at him. "I forgot how amazing this was. So"—she took a deep breath and closed her eyes—"relaxing."

Lillian looked calmer and more at ease. Better then she'd ever looked.

"It suits you," he said, taking a step toward her.

She glanced over at him and her expression grew serious. "Business meetings today?" She nodded toward his clothes.

"No. These are my relaxing clothes."

She folded her arms. "You're staying here?"

"Well, actually, we"—he motioned to his chest and then hers—"are expected at our wedding tonight."

Her eye widened. "Wedding?"

"Yeah. Mom wants us to do this before Mason ups his wedding date."

Lillian chewed her lip as she raised her hand and rubbed

the back of her neck. "Okay. Well, I guess it's probably better to just get it over with." The excited glint in her eye had disappeared.

Reed's heart squeezed a bit. He didn't want to upset her. For some reason, he had a desperate need to make her happy. He glanced over at her. "Hey, why don't we go out this morning? We're not needed until five, so we have plenty of time. We could go somewhere and spend some time away from everything. I could show you my version of a pottery studio?" He shrugged as she studied him. Was it terrible what he was asking?

She folded her arms. "What do you have in mind?"

His heart picked up speed. She didn't hate the idea of spending time with him. That was positive. "Why don't you take a shower and get ready. I'll arrange it all."

She tucked a loose strand of hair behind her ear and smiled. "Okay. That's probably a good idea."

He nodded as she passed by him. When she shut her door, Reed pulled out his phone from his back pocket to call Sondra, the housekeeper at his Hampton home.

She answered on the second ring. "Good morning, Mr. Williamson," she said.

"Sondra, I just wanted to let you know that I will be spending the morning and part of the afternoon there." He paused. "And perhaps the evening. Late." If Lillian loved the home as much as he did, she might want to spend the evening of their wedding there.

Sondra clicked her tongue. "Perfect. I will prepare the house. Will it be just you?"

Reed shook his head. "No. It will be me and my fiancée."

There was a choking sound on the other end. "Oh, congratulations, Mr. Williamson. Wow. That's amazing. I'm happy for you and Hannah."

"No. Not Hannah. Her name is Lillian." As he studied the doorframe that he was standing in front of, a strange feeling crept into his chest. Hearing Hannah's name did nothing for him. It was as if he'd forgotten about her. Besides the few mentions here and there from his mom, he hadn't thought of her once recently. Lillian had taken up more of his thoughts than anything else.

He swallowed as his emotions rose in his throat. What did that mean?

"Well, wonderful. I can't wait to meet her. I will have Jackson fix a few meals and leave instructions for you on how to prepare them. I'm guessing it will be a do-not-disturb situation?"

Reed's stomach lightened at what Sondra was implying. Thoughts of Lillian's smooth skin rushed into his mind. He cleared his throat when he realized that Sondra was expecting an answer. "Yes, that will be fine. Thank you."

"Of course, Mr. Williamson. The house will be ready for your arrival."

After they said goodbye, Reed hung up the phone and called his helicopter pilot. After he arranged their pickup,

Lillian emerged from her room looking refreshed. Her wet hair was pulled back in a low bun. She had on a bohemian style dress that hit her right below the knees. She was wearing a heart locket that accentuated the hollows of her neck. Reed couldn't help but stare at her. Every time he saw her, she got more and more beautiful.

As if sensing his approval, Lillian reached up and rested her hand where his gaze had lingered. She glanced over at him. "Cassie picked it out. It's not really my style," she said, pulling up the skirt a bit and moving it around.

"It should be. It looks as if that dress were made for you." Heat raced to Reed's cheeks as he pinched his lips shut. He hadn't meant for his voice to come out that low or for him to sound so intense. Hoping to make up for his blunder, he shot her a smile. "That's Cassie for you. She has a way of making everyone look amazing."

Lillian nodded as she slipped on a pair of sandals and shouldered a large bag. "Where are we going?"

Reed reached out and tucked his wallet into his back pocket. He grabbed his sunglasses and glanced over at her. "Do you have a swimsuit?"

"We're going swimming?"

He nodded. "Something like that."

Lillian studied him for a moment before she walked back to her room. She returned a few minutes later and patted her purse. "Got it."

He started walking toward the door but paused. "And we should probably bring your wedding dress. Just in case we are running late. We'll just have the helicopter drop us off at my grandfather's estate."

Lillian's eyes widened. "Helicopter?"

He followed her as they returned to her room to gather her dress, which was zipped up in a white garment bag. Reed draped it over his arm and grabbed the shoebox that Lillian dug out of her closet.

She had an uneasy expression on her face as he led her to the front door and opened it.

"Don't worry. Bert, my helicopter pilot, is the best in the business." He motioned toward the hallway with his head. When they got to the elevator, he pressed the up button.

"Wait. He's picking us up here?"

Reed nodded as he stepped into the elevator. "Yep."

Lillian let out her breath as she followed. The elevator rose the last few floors and stopped on the roof. It dinged, and the doors opened.

The whirring sound of Bert's helicopter filled the air. Wind blew all around them as they approached. Reed and Lillian ducked down as Bert waved for them to board.

Once they were buckled in with their headsets on, Reed glanced over at Lillian. Her eyes were wide, and her forehead was furrowed. Sensing her uneasiness, Reed reached out and wrapped his hand around hers.

She jumped as her gaze whipped to him. But before she pulled away, the helicopter rose, and Lillian grasped onto his hand with her left one. He laughed as she leaned closer to him, tipping her face toward his shoulder.

"You'll be fine," he said into the microphone.

She glanced over at him. He held her gaze, hoping she'd see that he meant it. She bit her lip and began to nod.

"Okay," she said.

He tried to keep his heart from pounding when she slowly turned her hand over so she could entwine her fingers with his. They held hands for the forty-minute ride to his house in the Hamptons. He almost complained when Bert descended onto the helipad located in the southern gardens.

For some reason, sitting with Lillian in silence during the ride had felt more right than any time he'd spent with Hannah. There was something about this woman next to him that was reeling him in. He was losing control of his feelings, and that thought made his stomach twist.

He couldn't do this. He couldn't have feelings for Lillian. She was his contract wife. There wasn't supposed to be any emotion there.

He needed to be smart and pull back. Put distance between himself and Lillian. Or he was going to be in trouble.

When they landed, Reed pulled his hand back and took off his helmet. Once he'd unbuckled, he helped Lillian with her equipment.

He clapped Bert on the back and motioned for him to return at four so they could make it to his grandfather's by five. Bert nodded in understanding, and then Reed hopped down from the helicopter.

After helping Lillian down, Reed grabbed her items and handed them to her. He gave the okay signal to Bert, who gave a thumbs-up and waited until Reed and Lillian moved far enough away so he could take off.

As soon as the rush of wind died down, Reed turned to find Lillian staring up at the Williamson's summer home. Reed hadn't been there in a long time. After Hannah broke up with him, it had become a place of bitter memories.

Maybe being here with Lillian would cure him of those. He nodded toward the large sliding doors that lined the house as he allowed hope to linger in his mind. Perhaps Lillian was just what he needed.

CHAPTER THIRTEEN

Lillian tried not to stare as Reed led her in through one of the sliding doors that made up the rear of what she could only assume was his home. He set her purse and dress down on a cream-colored couch and glanced back at her. She stood with her back against the door.

When was he going to realize that she wasn't the right person for this job? That he had way more to offer her than she did him? Then the memory of his mother holding a pen above the contract raced back to her. He hadn't asked her to this incredible beach home because he cared about her.

He probably had to. She hadn't been too studious about reading the contract, but it must have been a clause.

Take Lillian to your beach home to keep up the fake relationship.

She swallowed. Everything had to be in the contract. Why else would he be doing what he was?

The smiles. The looks. The brushes with his fingertips. It all had to be in preparation for their wedding later. There was no way any of this meant anything. He didn't want their touches in front of his family to be robotic and awkward. Practice was a necessity that he was getting out of the way.

"Are you thirsty? Hungry?" he asked as he made his way toward the large white kitchen that was located off of the room they'd just entered.

Everything was open and bright. Windows made up the front and back of the house. She could see the ocean on the other side as it lapped at the white, sandy beach.

"Sure," she said, slipping off her sandals and stepping tentatively into the home. This wasn't hers. Reed wasn't her husband. Her emotions were getting so out of hand that she needed to actually remind herself of this simple fact.

Especially since they'd spent the entire helicopter ride over here holding hands. She could still feel his skin against her own. She studied him as he made his way around the kitchen, grabbing bottles of water and a dish from the fridge.

There was no way any of the looks or touches meant anything to billionaire Reed Williamson. He was on a completely different playing field than her. He had assistants and housekeepers. He had a helicopter on standby for Pete's sake. She could barely make her rent or pay for the baby growing inside her.

She was a fool, and by the time this was all over, she was going to be broken. Again.

So, mustering all her confusing feelings, Lillian decided the best thing to do was ignore them and focus on completing her job. Stay married to Reed until the contract was fulfilled and then get as far away as she could. Maybe she could move out of his flat when the wedding was over. Didn't a lot of influential people do that? Live in separate homes from their spouses?

"You look worried." Reed's voice pulled her from her thoughts.

Lillian snapped her gaze over to him and swallowed. "Really? I'm not," she lied.

"Are you feeling okay? You know, since the helicopter ride seemed to freak you out." He pulled some foil back from the dish and glanced down, then pressed it back against the edge and put the dish in the oven.

She nodded as she pushed her previous thoughts from her mind and walked over to a barstool, where she settled in. She drummed the countertop with her fingers. "I'm not a big flyer."

He nodded as he leaned against the countertop. "Jackson made us up some filet mignon with cauliflower puree. I'm heating it up in the oven."

Lillian glanced behind him and then shrugged. "I was hoping to go swimming." Anything to get away from Reed and her confusing feelings. "Do you mind?"

His gaze met hers. His perfectly formed lips tipped up into a smile. "Of course not."

She nodded as she slid off the stool and grabbed her bag. "Bathroom?"

He tipped his head toward the far hall. "First door on the left."

She followed his instructions. Once she was in the bathroom, she let out the breath she'd been holding as she stared at herself in the mirror. She needed to get a grip. After she splashed some water on her face, she turned to her purse and pulled out the swimsuit that Cassie had picked out for her.

It had been wrapped in a cover-up, and when Lillian shook it loose, she let out a squeak. Cassie had bought her a skimpy, black one-piece. It had cutouts in the sides that made it look more like a bikini. This was so far out of Lillian's comfort zone, that she almost threw her dress back on. She could convince Reed that it was actually her swimming suit.

And then she felt like an idiot. What did it matter what she wore? Reed didn't care. It wasn't like he was attracted to her, and that was okay. She couldn't have a relationship with him anyway.

So she wrestled herself into the swimsuit and pulled the lacy cover-up over her head. At least it gave her some protection until she got down to the water. After she pulled her hair out of the bun, she shook it out, allowing it to fall in soft waves around her face.

She hung her dress up on the hook on the back of the door and then turned the handle. Just as she stepped out into the hall, she rammed right into Reed.

"Whoa," he said as he reached out and wrapped his arms around her waist to keep her from falling over.

Involuntarily, she reached out and grabbed onto his bare arms. When she turned her gaze forward, she found herself staring at Reed's very bare and very muscular chest. Her pounding heart carried heat to her cheeks. There was something so right about being held by Reed. It felt natural. Like she belonged there.

Despite her better judgment, she tipped her face up to look at him. His rich brown eyes shone with concern when he glanced down.

"Are you okay?" he asked, tightening his grip around her. Her breath caught in her throat as the sheer fabric of her cover-up allowed his body heat to warm her skin.

"I think so," she whispered. Every nerve in her body was going haywire. All she wanted was for him to dip her down and kiss her. To care about her, like she was trying hard not to care about him.

He leaned closer, his gaze dropping to study her lips.

Warning bells sounded in her mind, and even though her body ached to be held by Reed, she knew she needed to back away. This was not how she protected herself. She pushed back and cleared her throat. "Are you swimming as well?" she asked, nodding toward his teal trunks.

He pushed his hands through his hair. "If that's okay with you."

She hesitated and then nodded. Who was she to tell him

that he couldn't go swimming? This was his beach and his home. "Of course. Why wouldn't it be?"

He shrugged, and Lillian tried to ignore how his chest muscles flexed from the movement.

Not being able to stand the palpable silence between them, Lillian turned and made her way toward the kitchen. She grabbed a bottle of water off the counter and unscrewed the lid.

She could feel Reed's gaze on her as he approached. But instead of stopping next to her, he walked over to the oven and turned it off. "Don't want the food to burn," he said as he smiled over at her.

Lillian nodded as she took the opportunity to walk over to one of the large sliding doors and pull it open. The salty breeze surrounded her as she stepped out onto the deck. A large hot tub rose up to her left. A patio set that included a couch and chairs sat in the shade of a large, white umbrella. A multi-colored rug rested underneath it all.

She took a deep breath and glanced out toward the crystal-clear water. The white waves peaked just before the shore. Green grass danced in the wind. This place was paradise.

Lillian left her sandals on the deck and made her way down the stairs and onto the sand. It was warm but didn't burn her skin. It rose up between her toes and the sides of her feet as she walked through it.

When she got to the water's edge, she let it rush over her toes. It was cool against her warm skin. Feeling the need to dive into the water, she stripped off her swimsuit cover and dropped it on the sand.

The sound of Reed clearing his throat drew her attention over. Heat raced across her skin as she watched his gaze sweep over her body.

Blast, Cassie.

Not knowing what to do, she stood there, watching him.

"Wow," he said as he dropped an umbrella, blanket, and a pitcher of lemonade in the sand next to him.

"This isn't mine." The words tumbled from her mouth.

He quirked an eyebrow.

"Your sister bought it for me," she said, wrapping her arms around her stomach. Could he see the bump? Did he know? Why did she think it would be okay to wear a swimsuit that exposed that part of her body?

Reed nodded as he opened the umbrella and stabbed it into the sand. "Makes sense. That's Cassie's style." He squinted over at her. "For what it's worth, you look amazing." He shot her one of his mesmerizing smiles.

Butterflies erupted in her stomach as she dropped his gaze and glanced out to the ocean. Deciding that she didn't know what to say, she waded into the water. Once she was waist deep, she dove into the ocean, letting the temperature change shock her system.

When she popped back up, she glanced around, looking for Reed. But the shore was empty. Glancing around, she tried to find him. Suddenly, something grabbed her leg and she shrieked.

Reed popped up next to her with a smile on his face.

She splashed him and took a few steps back. "Way to scare the crap out of me."

A sheepish look passed over his face. "Sorry," he said.

Lillian smiled. "It's okay." His close proximity was scrambling the sensible part of her brain. Whenever she was around him, her heart took over, causing her to say and do dumb things.

"I mean it," he said, his expression growing serious. "I'm sorry for everything I said and did. Here"—he nodded toward the ocean—"and on the beach." He scrubbed his face with his hand. "I sounded like an idiot. And I apologize if I said the wrong thing. I promise, I'm not always this big of a dork."

Lillian eyed him. Why was he apologizing? "You didn't offend me," she said as she dipped down until the water rose to her neck.

A relieved expression passed over his face. "Thank goodness. I can't believe I said what I did. It's just when I'm around you..." His gaze met hers. "I forget how to be a functioning person."

Lillian parted her lips. It was nice to hear that he felt just as discombobulated around her as she did him. "It's weird, huh? There are moments that I feel so comfortable around you, and then other times..." She plugged her nose and went under the water. What was she doing? Why was she still talking? Getting emotionally involved with Reed was not what she was here to do.

Fake a relationship. Yes.

Nothing more.

When she broke the surface of the water, Reed was watching her. He had a contemplative expression on his face. She pushed her hair back and met his gaze.

"What?" she asked.

He dipped down until the water covered his shoulders. "Maybe we're trying too hard. What if we were to tell each other something personal about our past, which will help humanize each other?"

Lillian watched her hands as she moved them in the water in front of her. "Okay. You go first."

Reed scoffed and pushed his hands through his hair, spraying water around him. "I guess that's only fair. It was my idea after all." His expression grew serious as he focused on the water. "I was engaged once."

Lillian's heart picked up speed. He was telling her about Hannah. She swallowed as she studied him.

"I'm sure my mom or Cassie told you." He glanced over at her, and she shrugged. He groaned and muttered something about never keeping things quiet. "Well, I loved her, and she broke my heart." He swallowed, causing his Adam's apple to bob up and down. "Well, broke's not the best term. Ripped it from my chest. Pulverized it." He paused and then nodded. "Yeah. That sounds about right."

Lillian's heart squeezed at the thought of him hurting. What kind of fool did that to Reed? From what she knew, he was the kindest, most considerate person she'd ever met. Ten times better then Joshua.

"Thing is, she was seeing my half-brother on the side." He scrubbed his face with his hand. "He got her pregnant. And now, he just might take over the company that I've worked my whole life to build up, because of my grandfather's stupid stipulation that says I have to be married to become CEO."

Lillian watched as his expression went from anger to sadness. What a horrible year it must have been for him. It almost made her feel bad about wallowing in her depressing past.

"I was married," she said.

Reed's gaze shifted over to her. His eyebrows rose. "Married?"

She swallowed. What was she doing? Why was she getting emotionally involved with this man? That was the last thing she should do, and yet, she couldn't stop herself.

"His name is Joshua. I married him young. I thought we were perfect for each other." She sighed as she pressed on her stomach. "Apparently, we wanted different things. He wanted to be free and I held him back." Well, her and the baby. The memory of him staring her down, threatening her that if she didn't abort the baby, he would leave, rushed through her. She closed her eyes. It hurt too much to breathe right now.

The sound of Reed walking through the water caused her to open her eyes. He must do water aerobics because he was inches from her. The feeling of his hand surrounding her arm sent shivers across her skin.

"Lillian," he said. His voice was low, and she reveled in the sound of her name rolling off his tongue. He dipped down to meet her gaze. "That man is an idiot. Who plans his life without someone like you in it? He was a fool to let you go." He gave her a small smile.

Her heart hammered so hard in her chest that she thought it might explode. No man had ever talked to her like that. Or looked at her in such a way that made her believe that what he was saying was true.

And then a fluttering sensation raced across her stomach, bringing her back to reality. This wasn't real. None of this was. It was a contract. A legal document that needed to be fulfilled. And Reed knew how to accomplish his obligations. She was even starting to believe him.

She twisted her elbow, breaking contact with him. "You have to say that because you're my fake fiancé."

He parted his lips, and from the look on his face, he wanted to say something to contradict her. But she couldn't allow herself to stand here and listen. Instead, she dove into the water and swam away. She couldn't fall for Reed Williamson. And she was moments away from doing just that.

CHAPTER FOURTEEN

Reed stood in the water, watching Lillian as she swam away. His skin still tingled where he'd made contact with her. He ran his thumb over his fingertips. What was happening to him?

One minute he's complimenting her figure, and the next? Turning into some emotional buffoon, begging her to tell him her deep, painful secrets. He must really be losing his mind.

Letting out a growl, he dove into the water and began swimming. Anything to get his mind off his mistakes. Why had he said anything? He was obviously way more invested in this relationship then Lillian was.

Ugh. Even saying the word *relationship* made his stomach flip.

Hadn't he been the one to make the deal that they

weren't going to fall for each other? Leave it to him to be the one to break that pact.

Thirty minutes later, he stumbled onto shore. His legs and arms burned, but he felt more grounded. Nothing like adrenaline coursing through his veins to help clear his mind. It really was his grandfather's fault. Not allowing Reed to move on. Forcing a relationship on him.

If it wasn't for his grandfather, he would have stayed as far away from women as possible. Hide away in his office and drown himself in his work.

But because of this ridiculous stipulation, Reed found himself confused and tongue-tied around this beautiful woman, whom he was supposed to marry and pretend as if he loved her more than anything.

As he pushed through the sand, he saw Lillian lying on the beach. She'd brought one of the recliner deck chairs down from the house and set it up on the sand. Her hair was pulled up into a messy bun and she had on large sunglasses.

Reed couldn't help but let his gaze trail down the smooth lines of her body. Cursing himself, he pushed the water out of his hair and trudged up the beach.

"Where'd you go?" Lillian asked, shielding her eyes with her hand so she could glance over at him.

"I needed a swim," he said. She shifted, pulling up one of her legs while the other one lay flat on the chair. A very male feeling rushed through his body. He had half a mind to turn around and swim another half hour just to dispel the thoughts that were building up in his head.

He passed by her and up to the house, where he went straight into his room and jumped in the shower. At least here, Lillian couldn't distract him.

After a long hot shower, Reed dressed and made his way back to the kitchen. When he rounded the corner, he groaned. Lillian had made her way back up to the house and was now sitting at the bar. Thankfully, she was showered and dressed as well. No more siren swimsuit to muck up his brain. He was going to have a word with his sister when he saw her tonight.

Lillian turned when he entered the room. She was eating an apple. When she saw him, she covered her mouth with her hand. A sheepish expression crossed her face.

"I hope you don't mind that I helped myself," she said.

He shook his head. "Of course. Take what you need." He walked over to the oven and turned it on.

Before he could say anything, a phone rang. Lillian shifted around until she pulled her phone from her purse.

She glanced down at it and then over to Reed. "I'm going to take this outside," she said. Her skin was pale as she pressed the phone to her cheek and stepped outside, pulling the door shut behind her.

He tried to busy himself in the kitchen while Lillian paced the deck. She paused every so often, holding her stomach with her hand, and then a look of agitation would cross her face and she'd begin pacing again.

It took all his strength not to head out there to rescue

her. He wanted to tell off whoever was making her upset and pull her into his arms to comfort her.

He flexed his hands as he fought an internal battle. Thankfully, a few seconds later, she hung up. He watched her, hoping she'd come inside, but she didn't. Instead, she remained on the deck with her arms crossed in front of her. The wind blew, ruffling her skirt.

Unable to keep to himself, Reed forced each relaxed step as he made his way to the sliding door and out onto the deck.

"Food's almost ready," he said as he approached her.

Her gaze was fixed on the water in front of them. There was a sadness to her expression that squeezed his heart. She closed her eyes and nodded. "Thanks," she whispered. "I'm not that hungry."

He had to lean close to hear her before the wind picked up her words and whisked them away. Before he could stop himself, he opened his mouth and asked, "Is everything okay?"

She chewed her lip as she nodded, which slowly morphed into her shaking her head. "No. Joshua is looking for me."

"Your ex?"

She nodded. "Yes."

He leaned closer to her, placing his hand on the small of her back. He wanted her to know that he was there. That she could count on his support. There was no way this

Joshua character was going to hurt her again. "Why do you think he's looking for you?"

She turned toward him, putting her face only a foot away from his. She looked so small and fragile. His heart ached from the pain that emanated from her gaze. "He's seen whom I'm marrying." She nodded toward him. "At least that's my guess. And he wants in on it."

Anger boiled in his stomach. He knew what that was like. A person only caring for him because of how many zeros were in his bank account. He grasped her shoulders and turned his expression serious. "Lillian, look at me."

She raised her gaze until it met his.

"There is no way this man is going to bother you. He has nothing over you." He pulled her to his chest and wrapped his arms around her. "I won't let him hurt you," he said as he cradled her head in his hand.

A sob escaped her lips. "I just wish that my past would leave me alone," she said, her voice muffled by his shirt.

A sentiment he was all too familiar with. He pulled back so he could look down at her. She glanced up at him with red eyes. Letting his instinct take over, he reached down and wiped an escaping tear from her cheek. "That man is a fool to think that he could ever hurt you again. He doesn't know who he is messing with." He leaned closer to her. "Orson will bury him in legal fees if he thinks that he can get a penny from you." He needed her to know that he would take care of her—even if she were only his fake wife.

She hesitated. "No matter what?"

He laughed. There was nothing in her past that would allow Joshua to lay claim on anything Reed owned. The man was a fool to try to attempt anything. "No matter what." He met her gaze with as much force as he could muster.

"Thank you," she whispered, another tear slipping down her cheek.

He nodded, cradling her cheek in his hand and wiping the tear with his thumb. "You're going to be my wife in a few short hours. I will protect you. I promise." He let his gaze slip down to her lips. The only thought on his mind was how much he wanted to show her that she could trust him. His arms ached to pull her close and press his lips against hers.

She stiffened and pulled away. "I believe you," she said, wrapping her arms around her stomach and turning her gaze back to the ocean. "You're a good guy, Reed. Any woman would be lucky to have you as their real husband."

His heart squeezed as he watched her turn away from him. Why was she acting like this? Was he completely misreading what was happening between them? She seemed so happy one minute, just for her to push him away the next. Why couldn't he figure her out?

Perhaps he was a fool. Was he just wishing so hard that she cared about him, that he was seeing things that weren't there? He wouldn't put it past himself. He swallowed, forcing down his feelings. What an idiot he could be sometimes.

He needed to stop putting himself out there. Women

only broke his heart, and he couldn't let himself care for her, only to have her leave him.

He shoved his hands into his front pockets and nodded toward the kitchen. "Let's eat. Bert will be back in an hour to pick us up. We can get ready here, that way Bert can just drop us off at my grandfather's estate."

Lillian's shoulders rose as she took a deep breath. "Good idea." Then she hesitated. "You still want to go through with this?" She peeked over at him as if she feared what he was going to say.

He studied her. What kind of question was that? "Of course. Do you?"

Her cheeks hinted pink as she nodded slowly. "Yes. I just wasn't sure if my past was too much for you."

He scoffed. "I'm not one to judge on past relationships or less than stellar people in your life. Just look at my family." He ran his hands through his hair. "I'm not exactly related to the most put-together people."

A smile hinted on Lillian's lips and, despite Reed's better judgment, his heart soared. It was just what he needed to see. Lillian was perfection. And oh, how he wanted her to be his.

Feeling as if his emotions were getting the better of him, Reed nodded toward the kitchen. "Come on, let's eat."

They spent the remaining hour eating the filet mignon and talking. Reed couldn't help but feel mesmerized by the little things that Lillian did. The way her gaze softened when she talked about Tamara. Or the way her eyes crinkled when she laughed about the stupid things she did as a kid.

Everything about her put Reed at ease. He was starting to grow used to her company. The way her melodious laugh floated around him, the soft lines of her face when her expression grew contemplative. It was all drawing him in and taking hold of his heart.

She was so real, so raw. And so honest.

No woman he'd ever been with was anything like Lillian. Even though his mother had concocted a crazy plan, he was beginning to feel very grateful that she had. If not, Lillian would have never come into his life.

When they finished eating, they both leaned back in their chairs. Lillian's hand rested on her stomach.

"That was amazing," she said, smiling over at him.

Reed nodded as he wiped his mouth with his napkin. "Jackson knows what he's doing. He's in high demand on the island."

Lillian reached out and twisted her plate on the table. "I can see why."

Reed leaned forward. Before he could say anything, a beeping sound broke up the silence. Glancing down, he saw that it was a text from Bert. He was on his way to pick them up. He sighed and glanced over at Lillian.

"Bert's on his way. We should get ready."

Lillian placed the napkin next to her and scooted her chair back. Reed was out of his seat to help her the rest of the way. She stood and turned, her eyes wide.

She glanced down and chewed her lip. "You're going to have to stop doing that," she whispered.

He leaned in. It was beginning to feel like being here with Lillian was exactly what he needed. He wasn't sure he was going to be able to ever let her go. "Doing what?" He reached out and ran his finger across the back of her hand. Her skin was smooth.

She dropped her gaze to study the circles he'd begun to trace. Suddenly, she pulled her hand away. She clutched it to her chest with her other hand.

Silently, Reed cursed himself. What was he doing? Why did he keep letting his guard down? He shot her a smile, hoping she bought the lie.

She studied the floor before she glanced up at him. "You need to stop being so nice to me." She side-stepped him and headed toward the hallway. She'd left her things in a guest room.

He watched her retreat. "Lillian?" What was going on? He wasn't a fool. He knew what it looked like when a woman was interested in him. And Lillian acted like she was interested.

She turned, raising her hand to halt his words. "Reed, we can never be more then what we are. A contractual relationship that will end."

He walked toward her. Why was she saying this? "That can't be how you feel," he said.

Her forehead wrinkled as he stepped up to her. He dropped all inhibition and pulled her to him. She hesitated, but then relaxed when he glanced down at her.

"Lillian Brunette, I don't know why you keep pushing me away, but I'm going to tell you right now, I'm not Joshua. I will not leave you." He hesitated. "Unless you ask me to." He steadied his gaze. She had to know what he was feeling.

"But—"

He shook his head as he leaned closer to her. Her gaze dropped to his lips and then back up. "I want to kiss you," he said. All his emotions flooded to his throat, causing his voice to deepen.

"I—"

He shook his head again, cutting off her words. "But I won't. Not until tonight, when the priest pronounces us man and wife." He bent closer, and she tipped her face toward him. It was slight, but he reveled in the thought that she just might want to kiss him too.

Her hands were pressed against his chest. He wondered if she could feel his pounding heart. If she could, he was okay with that. For the first time, he didn't want to hide behind their fake relationship. He wanted her to know just what she was doing to him.

"Will you kiss me tonight?" he asked as he met her gaze.

Her eyes were wide as she studied him. Then her expression fell as she pressed her hands firmly on his chest and pushed away. "I should get ready," she said.

Reed allowed her to break the contact and step away. Even though this conversation hadn't given him the response he wanted, he wasn't going to give up hope. She had feelings for him. He could see it. She was as broken as he was—perhaps she just needed time. He could give that to her. "Of course," he said, nodding his head as he extended his hand toward the hall. "I'll see you when you're ready."

She hesitated and then turned toward the hall. Before she disappeared, she paused. "Reed?"

"Yeah," he said, glancing in her direction.

"Can I tell Tamara? I really need her at the wedding."

Worry floated into his mind, but he pushed it away. "If you think it's a good idea, then I'm okay with it."

She gave him a small smile. "Thanks."

He nodded. "Of course." Just as she disappeared, he whispered under his breath, "Anything for you."

He turned and headed toward his room. He had thirty minutes before Bert came.

Thirty minutes to think about what he'd done.

Thirty minutes to regret what he'd said.

And thirty minutes to hope that he hadn't just made a huge mistake.

CHAPTER FIFTEEN

Lillian paced the guest-room floor with her hand pressed against her stomach. This wasn't happening. Her emotions couldn't handle it.

But no amount of pushing her feelings down kept them from bubbling back up. She was beginning to care for Reed.

She groaned as she flopped down onto the bed. The down comforter puffed up around her as she sank into the pillowy material. Why did Reed have to be so comfortable and hypnotizing? He'd told her that he wanted to kiss her for real. Why wouldn't she let him?

Her fingers made their way to her bump. That was why. She was pregnant with another man's baby. Joshua's baby. She draped her elbow over her eyes. She was such an idiot to think that she could pull this off.

Tamara. She needed to talk to Tamara.

Sitting up, she reached over and grabbed her phone. Three rings and Tamara picked up.

"Hey, girl. I haven't heard from you in a few days. I was beginning to think that you had been kidnapped by Mr. Billionaire Bachelor." She laughed as if that was the funniest thing she'd heard all day.

"Tamara, I need a favor," Lillian said, flopping back down on her bed and covering her face with her hand.

"Is everything okay?" Tamara's tone had turned concerned.

"No. It's not." Lillian took a deep breath. "I need you to be my maid of honor."

Sputtering erupted on the other end of the call. It went on for a few seconds before Tamara cleared her throat. "What?" she asked.

"I'm marrying Reed Williamson." Before Tamara could respond, the whole story came tumbling out. The contract. The apartment. The pottery studio. The kiss. Everything. By the time she was done, it was so quiet on the other end that Lillian feared she'd lost the connection and would have to call Tamara back and tell her again.

"Are you still there?" she asked.

Tamara must have blown out her breath, because a whooshing sound caused Lillian to pull the phone away from her ear.

"This... Is... Incredible!" Tamara's voice went from quiet to loud.

Lillian stared at the phone. Had her best friend not

heard her right? "How is this incredible? I have to marry a man who might have feelings for me, while I'm carrying the baby of the man who dumped me. Oh, and Joshua has decided that this would be the perfect time to come waltzing back into my life." Ugh, this was a huge mess. One giant doozy.

Tamara tsked. "Seriously? You have a billionaire fawning after you, and you're worried about Joshua? That man is an idiot. I wouldn't worry about him." She sighed. "But you have to do something about the baby. You have to tell Reed. Before this gets too far."

Lillian's stomach twisted. She couldn't do that. For so many reasons. What if she had the baby early and it passed away? She couldn't deal with that again. Especially if other people knew.

Then an equally painful thought entered her mind. What if Reed found out and broke off the contract because she hadn't told him? Could she really handle being rejected by two men because of a pregnancy?

"I can't, Tamara. I can't tell him." She buried her face into the comforter. However she looked at the situation, she came out brokenhearted.

"Lil, you have to. You can't marry the man and keep this a secret. I know you think that you're going to lose this baby, but what if you don't? How are you going to explain the tiny human that suddenly appears a few months from now?"

Lillian shook her head. Tamara didn't understand. The

time she'd spent with Reed had been the best she'd ever experienced. Was she really going to be able to walk away?

Her stomach flipped. She was going to vomit. Rolling off the bed, she dropped the phone and sprinted to the bathroom. After all of Jackson's hard work was in the toilet, she sat back. Tears brimmed her lids as she cradled her head in her hands. Everything was a mess. A gigantic mess.

Tamara had hung up by the time she got back to the phone. Not feeling rushed to call her back, Lillian took the time to get a grip on her emotions. She made her way back into the bathroom, where she washed her face and patted it dry.

Once she felt more human, and less like she was going have a complete breakdown, she picked up her phone and dialed Tamara, who answered on the first ring.

"Did you throw up?" she asked instead of a greeting.

Lillian sighed. "Yes."

"See? The baby is telling you that you need to fess up. Tell Reed what's going on."

Lillian shook her head as she dabbed under her eyes. "No. I can't." She let out the breath she'd been holding. "The pregnancy won't last, so it wouldn't matter anyway. I can't risk telling him, just to lose the baby." She felt tears brim her lids again, so she took a moment to push her feelings down. She could do this.

Tamara was silent for a moment before she sighed. "Okay. Do whatever you want to do. I don't agree with it, but I'll support you."

A weight felt as if it was lifted off her chest. That was what she needed. Her best friend. "Thanks. And I understand. I'll think about telling Reed, but right now I need to focus on marrying him." She was actually grateful that she didn't have a choice there. She had to marry him, whether she wanted to or not. It was nice to have that decision made. It gave her a goal to work toward.

"Sounds good. What do you need me to do?"

After giving Tamara the details of the evening, Tamara agreed to meet her at Reed's grandfather's house, dressed in a maid-of-honor gown and a smile. They hung up just as a knock sounded on Lillian's door. She glanced at the clock. She was late. Bert must be here, and she wasn't even ready.

She walked over to the door and pulled it open. Reed was standing on the other side with his arm propped up on the frame, staring down at her. He had a strong, sexy man vibe to his stance. She swallowed as she tried not to let her gaze linger on him for too long. Why did guys stand like that? Did they know it drove women crazy? Forcing down her hormones, she smiled up at him.

A concerned expression passed over his face. "Are you okay? Were you crying?"

She turned, discreetly blotting her eyes and took in a deep breath. "No. I wasn't crying. I'm just tired. I think the sun really zapped me of energy."

Reed pushed off the doorframe and entered the room. "Are you sure? I could ask Mom to push the wedding back a day."

Lillian took a deep breath and turned. "No. No worries. I'll be fine. I'm sure your mother went to quite a lot of trouble for this. I would hate to disappoint her."

Reed studied her and then nodded. "You're right. It's probably better that we do this tonight. Before anyone changes their mind."

Lillian walked over to the closet and pulled out the dress. After she gathered her other things, she turned, only to find Reed standing right behind her with his arms outstretched.

"Can I help?" he asked.

Lillian glanced down at his hands. She hesitated and then nodded. He could help her. It wouldn't kill her to let him do that.

He draped the dress across his arm and clutched her bag in his hand. He looked grateful that she'd allowed him to help. He smiled at her. "Are you ready?"

"Yes," Lillian said, although every part of her told her that was a lie. She wasn't ready for any of this. She had so many concerns, and some of them stemmed from the fear of what this relationship might do to her. Others were worries about what she might do to Reed. He was entering into a marriage, thinking he knew her. When the truth was, there was so much about her that he didn't know.

"It's in the contract, right?" she asked, hoping to dispel the guilt she felt about lying to him.

He glanced down at her. "Contract?"

"Yeah. I have to marry you because it's in the contract."

All she wanted was for him to say that it was her duty. That she was in breach of her word if she backed out. That she had to stay. There was no other option.

He hesitated as they walked through the living room toward the sliding doors that led to the back gardens, where Bert was waiting for them. She could see him moving in the distance. When she glanced up at Reed, he was watching her.

"If you don't want—"

"Reed, just tell me I have to. That's all I need to hear."

He looked confused for a moment, then a stony expression settled on his face. He had finally realized what she was asking him. If he said she didn't have to, there was a good chance she would walk out the door, taking all his hopes of owning the company with her. There was no other reason for her to stay.

He took a deep breath and glanced out the window. "Yes. You are contractually obligated to marry me and stay married until my grandfather passes away or signs the company over to me. If you leave, you will be in breach of that agreement and Williamson Industries will have no other choice but to exercise its rights as they pertain to the contract." He sounded like a recording of a lawyer. His grip tightened on her things. "Is that what you needed to hear?" He hesitated. "Is that the only reason you're here? Why you're staying?"

Lillian fought back the tears. She couldn't show Reed that everything he'd just said was breaking her heart. It wasn't fair to involve him in her mess. So she mustered a confident look and turned to him. "Of course. Why else would I be here?"

Not waiting for his answer, she took off down the lawn toward the helicopter. Thankfully, they had a fifteen-minute ride inside the noisy cockpit. Hopefully, Reed would get the hint and leave her alone. Right now, she was pretty sure her heart was crumbling from her own words.

Bert readied the helicopter as Reed climbed in. Lillian's stomach flipped from Reed's tense brow and clenched jaw. She'd hurt him. Bad. Hopefully, this meant that he was pulling away from her. That he'd keep his distance and not fall in love with her. Because right now, she was moments away from falling for him.

The ride to Reed's grandfather's house was quiet and uncomfortable. Lillian kept her gaze trained out the window on the scenery that passed by underneath them. Her mind was racing, and she tried to calm it. Reed's reaction was good. It was what she wanted.

Bert said something about them landing in a few minutes, so Lillian glanced outside as they passed by the island. The house looked different from up in the air. She could see that it was situated in the middle of a huge lot with trees lining the outside. A helicopter pad sat on the outskirts of the property, with a limo parked next to it.

The sun was low in the sky, casting long shadows from the trees across the grass. As soon as Bert landed, Reed unbuckled and pulled his helmet from his head. He glanced over in Lillian's direction, and she tried to ignore the hurt in his gaze as he waited for her to do the same.

When she was ready, he jumped from the helicopter and extended his hand to help her down. Her heart squeezed from the fact that even though she'd rejected him over and over again, he was still a gentleman, putting her needs above his own.

She took his hand, trying to ignore the feelings that raced across her skin from his touch. She tried to ignore just how good it felt to be held by him. How everything in her life seemed to fit into place when he was around.

Get a grip, Lillian. She scolded herself.

This wasn't keeping her distance. This wasn't protecting her heart. This was jumping in with two feet, just like she'd done so many times in the past. How else had she gotten to her current situation?

Once she was on the ground, she dropped his hand and took her items from Bert as he handed them down. She gave Bert a smile and headed toward the house. Anywhere was better than right next to Reed.

When she climbed the back stairs and walked across the large deck that led up to the house, she heard footsteps thudding behind her. She turned around to see Reed racing to catch up with her. He had a clothing bag draped over one arm and it flapped around as he ran.

"You're fast," he breathed out. He hunched over and took in a few gulps of air. "From what you said earlier, I figured that I might have to drag you in there." He glanced up at her as if he wasn't sure how she was going to react.

She hesitated. What was she supposed to say to that? Of course she was going to follow through with her word. "I—that's not who I am. I said I'll marry you, and I will."

Reed studied her and then a sheepish look passed over his face. "I'm sorry. I didn't mean to imply that you wouldn't. Of course you are a woman of your word." He steadied his gaze as he met hers. It was as if he were trying to tell her that he trusted her. Despite all she'd done, he still cared for her.

She couldn't handle the heartbreak that squeezed her chest. "Let's get up there and do this," she said, nodding toward the house.

Reed ducked down as he walked past her. "Of course."

Once they got to the large double doors, he reached out and turned the handle. Just as she passed by him, he reached out and pressed his hand onto her lower back and guided her in. Shivers raced across her skin from the heat of his touch. This was not good. Oh, this was not good.

Reed followed after her, shutting the door behind him. Two steps into the house and a squeal sounded. Lillian glanced up to see Cassie racing up to her. She wrapped her arms around Lillian and pulled her close.

"I'm so happy you guys are finally here!" she said, placing a kiss on each cheek before pulling back. "It took you two long enough." She raised her eyebrows suggestively.

Reed made a disgruntled sound. “Is everyone here?” he asked, reaching out and hugging Cassie.

“If you mean Mason and that snake, Hannah, then no, they’re not here. And mom thinks that they aren’t going to come, so we should be in the clear.”

Lillian watched as Reed nodded, but then his tanned complexion paled. Before she knew what she was doing, she reached out and rested her hand on his forearm. “It’s okay. We are going to do this. He will not win.” She gave him a reassuring smile.

Reed’s gaze dropped to her hand and then back up to her. It seemed that her gesture had its intended affect. A wave of confidence passed over his face. “Thanks,” he said.

Lillian nodded, keeping her hand on his arm. Butterflies erupted in her stomach. She swallowed, hoping that would calm them.

“Okay, you two love birds, save the touching for tonight,” Cassie said as she pulled on Lillian’s arm.

Reed shot her an annoyed look. “Come on, Cas,” he said.

Cassie shrugged as she pulled Lillian away. “I gotta go dress up your bride!” she called.

Lillian allowed Cassie to lead her through the house. Dark wood covered the walls, banisters, and floors. A deep red rug ran the length of the hallway. Their footsteps were muted by the plush material.

Cassie stopped at a door and turned the handle. “Let’s get you ready,” she exclaimed and pushed the door open.

CHAPTER SIXTEEN

Cassie ushered Lillian into the room and shut the door behind them. After a quick scan, she pronounced that Lillian was a mess and she was going to have to start from scratch.

"Shower," she commanded, pointing to the door along the far wall.

Lillian nodded and headed to the bathroom. Cassie had on a no-nonsense expression, so Lillian thought it was probably best to do as she was told.

When she was clean, she stepped out of the shower and wrapped towels around her body and her hair. She opened the door, letting the steam escape in heavy wisps.

Cassie was waiting a few steps away with her arms crossed. "That took forever," she said.

Before Lillian could respond, Cassie had grabbed her elbow and pulled her over to a chair in front of a lighted vanity. After drying, curling, and tugging, Cassie managed to wrangle Lillian's hair into soft ringlets around her face. Then Cassie moved on to Lillian's makeup.

Ten minutes later, Lillian almost didn't recognize the woman staring back at her. She looked sophisticated and elegant. Everything that Lillian had never believed she could be.

"Cas, you did an amazing job," she said, turning to see Cassie's beaming face.

Cassie shoved her shoulder. "It helps when I have a beautiful canvas to work on."

Lillian's heart swelled. Cassie had been nothing but nice to her. And yet, Lillian had kept the truth about the baby from her. What kind of friend did that? Pushing the thoughts of her betrayal from her mind, Lillian turned, forcing herself to focus on getting married.

"Let's get the dress on. We're wanted in ten minutes," Cassie said as she walked over to the bed and picked up the dress.

Lillian nodded, taking the hanger from her and heading back into the bathroom.

After discarding her towel, she started to slip on her bra and underwear. There was a knock on the bathroom door.

"I forgot something," Cassie called.

Grabbing her towel, she wrapped it around her body and opened the door. Cassie was standing on the other side with an inscrutable expression. In her outstretched hand was a white bag. "Something a little fun and maybe scandalous," she said.

Lillian shot her a look as she grabbed the bag and shut the bathroom door again. Flashbacks of the swimsuit raced back to her. "What did you do?" she called through the door as she pulled out a pair of white undies and a matching bra.

"Just something for the wedding night," Cassie called back.

Lillian choked as she pulled out a garter belt and thigh-highs. "Seriously?"

Cassie laughed. "Just having fun."

Lillian's heart picked up speed as she imagined what Reed would do if he saw her in this. Emotions raced through her that she was not ready for. Stuffing the lingerie back into the bag, she set it on the vanity—as far away from her as possible. There was no way she could wear that. Not with the way she was feeling.

There was a knock on the bedroom door, followed by muffled voices. Lillian dressed in her own undergarments and turned to the dress hanging on the back of the door. She flipped it around so the back faced her and unzipped it. Shaking it out, she slipped into it and pulled it up.

Once her arms were through the sleeves, she turned and caught a glimpse of herself in the full-length mirror. Her breath caught in her throat as she inspected her reflection. It was a mermaid-cut dress completely covered in lace. The heart-shaped neckline could be seen underneath the lace that covered her shoulders and made tiny cap sleeves. It had an elegant and classy look to it.

Just her style. Cassie had done an amazing job.

She pulled the zipper up as high as she could and then turned to the door. Just as she twisted the handle, a knock sounded.

"Lil, are you okay?" Tamara asked.

Relief flooded Lillian's chest. Her best friend was here. She pulled open the door and wrapped her up in a hug. It felt so good to see someone she knew.

Tamara let out a whoosh of air when Lillian squeezed her.

"Wow," Tamara said, pulling back and looking at Lillian. "You've never been this excited to see me." She smiled. "You look amazing," she said, stepping back and inspecting her.

"Thanks," Lillian said.

Cassie approached from behind and slid the zipper up the rest of the way. "You're going to knock Reed's socks off," she said, wrapping her arm around Lillian's shoulders.

That was the last thing she wanted to do. Maybe she should go back into the bathroom and refuse to leave until they had a black garbage bag for her to wear. But then Reed's disappointed expression entered her mind. No matter how scared she was about any of this, she couldn't let him down. Not after all he'd done for her.

So she smiled over at Cassie and Tamara. "Where are my shoes?"

REED STOOD in one of his grandfather's guest rooms, feeding his cufflinks through his sleeves. He was standing in front of the mirror, but he wasn't looking at anything in particular. Instead, his thoughts kept returning to Lillian. How close they'd gotten, just to have her pull back.

Was he being a fool? Did she really not care about him? There were moments when he thought that perhaps, she had felt something, too. But those moments only lasted for a few fleeting seconds before she'd throw up a wall and push him away.

It was all so confusing. Especially, when all he wanted to do was take her into his arms and make her his.

"Nervous?" Johnson, his business partner and best man, asked. He was sitting on the bed, rolling a lint brush against his tux.

Reed glanced at him in the mirror and then back at his own reflection. Why wasn't he nervous? He knew he should be, but he wasn't. He had begun to care for Lillian, and if marrying her meant he could spend more time with her, then so be it. He was ready for this. More ready then he'd ever felt about anything else in his life.

"Nah," he said, grabbing the other cufflink and threading it through. "I've got this."

Jackson nodded as he stood and walked over to the dresser on the far wall. A chime sounded, but it didn't sound like his ringtone, so Reed paid it no mind. His thoughts were plagued with Lillian. Not much else held his attention.

Johnson picked up his phone and studied it. A few seconds later, a newscaster's voice filled the room.

"That's right, ladies and gentlemen, I have it on good authority that tonight, Mr. Reed Williamson—Mr. Billionaire Bachelor himself—is getting hitched!"

A cheer rose up.

Reed's stomach dropped. He zeroed in on Johnson's phone, reaching out to take it. A woman with a blonde bob was standing in front of a huge crowd just outside of his building. Lights were directed at the front doors where Harold was trying desperately to get them to leave. His bald head was sweating as he waved like a wild man at the cameras.

The reporter took no note of his desperation, instead she approached him and shoved the microphone in his face. "Is Reed here?" she asked, turning to smile back at the camera.

"You must leave. This is private property," Harold huffed out. He mustered an intimidating look, but the reporter didn't seem fazed.

"Are you saying that Reed Williamson is not home right now?"

Harold's face flushed red as he sputtered a few times.

"If he is not here, where is Mr. Williamson?" She turned to the audience who all booed and made sad faces. There were a few muffled sentences before the woman shot her bright white smile back at the camera. "The

Williamson estate," she exclaimed, and the video feed went black.

Reed scrolled down. There had already been over a half a million views of this YouTube video and it had only been live for just under an hour. That was enough time for the reporters to arrive.

Reed shoved Jackson's phone into his friend's hand and walked over to the windows. Pulling back the drapes, he saw that the front of the estate was lined with reporters. Apparently, the popularity of the video had brought the attention of every major news station in the state.

Reed swore under his breath. Who had told them? This wasn't the small wedding he'd wanted. The last thing he needed was a huge story that mucked up his plans.

He grabbed his tuxedo coat and headed out of the room. There was no time like the present to speed up this wedding. As long as his grandfather witnessed the marriage, then he should be in the clear. He'd get the company, and everything would finally be right in the world.

Well, almost right. Without Lillian, Reed was beginning to think that his life was never going to be complete. Then the thought that they'd be married entered his mind. If she didn't love him now, he'd make a point of getting her to fall in love with him eventually.

Lillian had filled his mind and taken a hold of his heart. She was everything to him. No other woman had trusted him so completely like she did. She was honest and kind. He'd never felt as if she'd been interested in his money. She was genuine, and he couldn't wait to spend more time with her.

He stood outside the room that the ladies were getting ready in. He swallowed as he raised his hand to knock.

After a few seconds, Cassie appeared in a baby-pink chiffon dress. Her hair had been pulled up. She looked amazing.

"Wow, Cas. You clean up nice."

She feigned a modest expression that morphed into a smile. "I know," she said.

He studied her. "Is Lillian ready?"

She shot him an excited look. "Yes," she said as she pushed the door open to reveal Lillian standing there.

Reed's heart picked up speed. It felt as if it was going to leap from his chest. There had been very few times when he'd felt stunned speechless and this was one of them. He parted his lips to say something, but nothing came out.

Lillian's eyebrows rose.

"You look amazing," he said. The white lace contrasted against her skin. Her red hair had been curled and fell over her shoulders. The words that he was trying to form in his mind paled in comparison to how she actually looked.

"Thanks," she said. Then she reached down and pressed on her stomach.

Reed wondered if it was her nerves that made her look flushed.

Suddenly, she wavered, tipping to the side. Reed stepped forward, catching her before she collapsed onto the ground. Worry raced through him. Scooping her legs up, he held her to his chest.

"Are you okay?" he asked, glancing down at her.

She swallowed and nodded as she rested her head on his shoulder. "I think I just need to lie down for a minute."

Reed walked her over to the bed and laid her on it. Tamara was right behind him and waved him away.

"Give her some space," she commanded.

Not wanting to leave her side, but also not wanting to overwhelm her, Reed listened to his grandfather's nurse who had come into the room and stepped out of the way.

After Lillian's vitals were taken, Tamara instructed him to get her a glass of water. Reed started to protest, but from the expression on Tamara's face, he just pinched his lips together and made his way out of the room.

Just as he reached the bottom of the stairs, his mother appeared. She was wearing a dark purple sequin dress and an expectant look.

"Well, where is she?" she asked.

Reed shot her a look. Nothing was more important than making sure Lillian was okay. Not the company, not the money. Something was wrong with her. He could feel it, and he wasn't going to let his mother pressure Lillian into walking down the aisle just to please her.

"Not now, Mother." He walked past her and into the kitchen, where he grabbed a few bottles of water from the fridge.

His mother was hot on his heels. "Did you see the

reporters?" she asked, walking over to the windows and peering out.

Reed scoffed. "You act so surprised. Weren't you the one who called them?"

His mother turned around with her eyes wide. "I did not. Sure, I wanted the engagement publicized, but not this."

Reed stacked the bottles in his arm and moved to head back upstairs. "Is everything a show for you? Don't you care about what this might do to Lillian? To me?" If anything happened to her, he would never forgive his mother. He cared too much for Lillian to let her suffer.

His mom reached out and rested her hand on his arm. "What are you talking about? Of course I want what's best for you. Why else do you think I arranged this? It's not every mother's dream to marry her son off to a woman she barely knows."

Reed hesitated and turned to look at his mom. She had a point. Neither of them wanted the situation that they were in right now. He needed to remember that.

Sensing his understanding, his mom reached out and pulled him into a hug. "I love you, Reed. We're family. We always have each other's best interest in mind."

He sighed and nodded, wrapping his mom in a side hug. "You're right. And, honestly, Lillian feels more like family then Hannah ever did. She needs me. I have to be there for her."

His mom nodded into his shoulder. "Then go, take care

of her. If you need me to, I'll cancel the wedding. It's more important to make sure she's okay."

Reed leaned down and kissed his mom on the head. "Thanks, ma." Pulling away, he made his way to the stairs. "I'll let you know," he said as he disappeared at the top.

CHAPTER SEVENTEEN

Something wasn't right. It wasn't right at all.

A sharp pain in her lower back had started small and intermittent. But it was building to the point that when it happened, it took her breath away. Memories of going into labor months ago flashed back to her. It was happening again. She could feel it.

Tamara leaned in to whisper, "What's going on?"

Lillian shot her a pained expression. One that said she was hurting in more ways than just the physical. Thankfully, Tamara understood.

"Do you want to go to the hospital?"

Lillian swallowed. She didn't want to. Bad things happened when she went there. She'd walked in pregnant and came out alone. But this pain was starting to radiate down her legs, and she knew something was wrong. So she bit her lip and nodded.

Tamara went into nurse mode. She stood and made her way over to Cassie where they talked in hushed tones.

Reed appeared in the doorway with a worried expression. He had half a dozen bottles of water tucked in his arms. When he saw her, his brow creased. She must have looked like a mess, from his reaction.

He walked right by Lillian and Cassie and dumped the water onto a chair next to the bed. Then he approached, hesitantly at first, but then he reached down and grabbed her hand. He sat on the bed and met her gaze.

"Are you okay?" he asked, sweeping his gaze over her.

She nodded then winced as another sharp pain squeezed her stomach. She clamped her eyes shut and breathed through it. When the pain passed, she glanced up at him.

"What's happening? How can I help?" He reached out and rested his hand on her cheek.

"Reed?" Tamara asked.

He turned.

"We need to take her to the hospital."

Reed sputtered as he stood. Lillian stared at Tamara who had her eyes wide. There was no way she wanted Reed to know about the baby. Not now. Not when she was about to lose it.

"Hospital? Why?" He turned to look at Lillian.

She shot him a comforting smile. "It's just a precaution. I'm sure I'm fine." When she moved her gaze to meet Tamara, her friend pursed her lips and leaned toward her.

Lillian knew she wanted her to tell Reed, but she couldn't. So she steeled her expression, hoping that her best friend read it and knew what it meant.

Thankfully, Tamara sighed and turned to Reed. "I should take her."

"I'm going," he said as he started to pace.

"No. It's okay. Tamara can take me. I don't want to inconvenience you."

Reed stopped and whipped around to stare at her. "Inconvenience me? Are you serious? You were about to become my wife."

Lillian winced at his words. She hated how much her heart swelled at his intensity when he spoke them. And at this moment, that was what she wanted. She wanted to be his wife. She wanted for him to care for her in a way that no man ever had in her past. She wanted him to be her family—she just didn't know how to tell him.

And if he found out that she'd lied to him, that would be it. Could he ever forgive her?

So she pinched her lips shut and gathered her strength. "Reed, I want to do this alone. Please." Hoping her emotions didn't give her away, she met his gaze.

He studied her for a moment, and a hardened expression passed over his face. "Okay. If that's what you want."

She nodded, and Tamara stepped up to him. "Can we take your helicopter?"

Reed glanced over at her and nodded. "Of course."

Lillian let out the breath she'd been holding. Part of her

was dreading what was coming and the other part welcomed it. She was ready for answers. So much of her life lately had been spent holding her breath, waiting for this exact moment, but not knowing when it would happen.

As much as it pained her heart to lose the baby, she welcomed that pain. It was something she was familiar with.

Reed stepped out of the room as Tamara and Cassie helped her change out of her dress and into some comfortable clothes. Lillian tried not to wince as she hobbled toward the door. Reed leaned against the wall, staring into the room as she approached. She met his gaze, and her heart squeezed in her chest.

He was hurting. Bad.

How selfish could she be? She'd allowed herself to do the exact thing she'd told herself she would never do. Lead Reed to believe that something could happen between them. What kind of selfish person did that?

As she took a step toward him, an intense pain shot through her stomach, taking her breath away. She stumbled, grabbing onto the wall for support.

Reed was to her side before she could even blink. He wrapped his arms around her and pulled her to his chest. She opened her lips to protest but saw the ache in his eyes.

"How are you feeling?" he asked. His voice was deep and full of concern.

Lillian chewed her lip as she shrugged.

He scoffed. "Why are you lying to me?" he asked.

Tamara waved for him to follow her out to the hall.

Lillian wanted to wiggle from his grasp so he would put her down, but from the grip he had on her, he wasn't going to let her go anytime soon.

She took a deep breath and let him carry her down the stairs to the front door. He glanced down at her as if he was still waiting on a response.

"Reed, I just think it's best for us to keep our distance. There are things about me that you don't know." Her voice dropped as emotion filled her throat. "That you can't know."

She watched as Reed's jaw muscles twitched. He tightened his grip as he carried her outside. When they stepped out onto the front stoop, a cheer rose up from the reporters that were in the distance. Reed paid them no mind as he stared down at Lillian in an open and unabashed way.

"So you're saying that everything we've gone through. All the feelings I've had, are what? A lie?"

Lillian's heart swelled at his words. *Feelings he's had.* Did that mean what she thought it did? But it couldn't. Not when she wasn't worthy of his love. So she pushed her feelings away and lied.

She nodded. "Yes."

She kept her gaze focused on her hands as she felt his gaze on her. But she couldn't look. She couldn't acknowledge what her words had done to him. Not now. Another pain passed through her, and she tightened from the pressure. They were coming faster now.

What was she going to do? As much as she wanted to think that she'd prepared for this, she hadn't. A deep sadness settled in around her as realized what all of this meant. She fought the tears on her lids. Why had she allowed herself to hope? To love? Clearing her throat, she breathed out the tension.

Reed kept her in his arms until they got to the helicopter. Lillian was grateful for the whooshing sound from the blades that would drown out any conversation he would try to have with her. Once she was strapped in, he stepped back.

As she watched him retreat, she fought the urge to call to him. To have him come back and stay by her side. She'd grown accustomed to his presence. What was she going to do when he was gone?

And then she chided herself for sounding so selfish. What was she going to do? What about Reed? He'd entered into a contract with a woman who'd lied to him. Who'd kept a deep secret from him. A woman who could never be his family. Who just took and had nothing to give.

He was better off without her.

So she dropped her gaze and waited as Tamara boarded. Then Bert took off. Once they were far enough away, she glanced down to see that Reed had not moved from his spot. She could tell his face was tilted up, watching them leave.

Now alone, a sob escaped her lips. She was losing everything. Reed. The baby. Anyone who would ever think of her as family would be out of her life in moments. And then what was she going to do?

Tamara glanced over at her. Sympathy washed over her countenance.

"It's not too late," she said through the headset microphone.

Lillian shook her head. "Yes it is. It's all too late." She wiped her tears as another contraction came. Hunching over, she breathed through the pain.

Once it was over, she swallowed. If only she could somehow breathe through the pain of a broken heart, she just might be able to survive this evening.

They landed on the helicopter pad of New York Presbyterian hospital. As soon as Bert opened the door, a stretcher appeared. Before Lillian had time to think, she was strapped to it and wheeled inside.

A nurse was shouting at her, and she was trying as hard as she could to answer her questions. Thankfully, Tamara was there, spouting all the facts for her. Right now, Lillian hurt so bad, she could barely breathe.

When they got her to Labor and Delivery, the realization of what was happening settled in around her. She was going to lose a baby. Again.

She squeezed her eyes shut as she tried to push out all of her fears and calm her mind.

"How are you feeling?" a deep voice asked.

Lillian glanced up to see that a doctor had come in. He was staring at her chart and then over to her.

"How long until this is all over?" she asked. She needed

an ending point, or she just might not make it through the night.

"That's what we are going to try to avoid." He grew silent as he studied the clipboard. "It looks like you are only a centimeter dilated, so that's a good sign. We've given you some terbutaline in your IV to stop the contractions. I suspect these started because of dehydration and stress."

She swallowed. That very well could be. She'd been so overwhelmed with what she was going to do about Reed and the baby, that she'd forgotten to take care of herself.

Another contraction came, this time calmer than the previous ones. She glanced up to see the doctor studying her.

"Are they getting easier?"

She let out a breath and nodded. "Yes."

He smiled. "Good. The nurse will be back in to do an ultrasound so we can get an accurate due date." He hesitated. "It says in your chart that this isn't your first pre-term baby."

Pain squeezed her chest as she nodded. "Yes. I had one last year."

A knowing expression passed over his face. "I understand. We will do what we can to make sure that it won't happen again."

Lillian nodded as she dropped her gaze. Thankfully, Tamara came in and the doctor excused himself. She smiled over at Lillian.

"How are you feeling?" she asked, walking over and sitting on the chair next to the bed.

Tears welled up in her eyes. "What am I going to do?"

Tamara reached out and grabbed her hand. "Don't worry. They'll take care of you and the baby. Plus, if they do have to deliver, babies have survived at twenty-plus weeks."

Lillian nodded. "You're right. Positive thinking."

There was a quiet knock on the door. Lillian turned and said, "Come in." It must be the nurse with the ultrasound equipment. If she were honest with herself, the thought of seeing the baby excited her. Being here made this real.

"How are we feeling?" a portly nurse asked as she wheeled in an ultrasound machine. She smiled over at Lillian. "Better when I tell you that your husband is in the hall." She wiggled her eyebrows.

Lillian's breath caught in her throat. "What?" Reed was here? He actually came?

"Yeah. He's right outside. I told him I'd check with you first and then let him in. Is that okay?"

Lillian shifted in the bed to pull herself up. After she adjusted the blanket, she nodded. "Let him in."

"Come on in," the nurse called, disappearing around the corner.

Lillian held her breath as she waited. It felt like an eternity until Joshua appeared from the hall.

Wait. Joshua?

Frustration boiled up inside of her. "What are you doing

here?" she asked, folding her arms across her chest. She needed to protect herself.

Tamara stood and glared at him. "You need to leave."

The nurse stood there with her lips parted. "Is he not the father?"

Lillian scoffed in unison with Tamara.

"That's the father. He just gave up his right to be called that when he walked out," Tamara said, placing her hands on her hips.

Joshua wrung his hands as he glanced between all the women. "Can I talk to you?" he asked, stepping forward and focusing on Lillian.

Right now, Lillian wanted to chase everyone from her room so she could nurse her broken heart in peace. But that wasn't realistic. And from the apologetic look on Joshua's face, she realized that she was too tired. Carrying this much pain and stress was exhausting. So she nodded and glanced over at Tamara.

"Give us a minute."

Tamara's lips fluttered like a fish out of water. "But—"

"It'll be okay," Lillian said, reaching out and squeezing her best friend's hand.

Tamara's face reddened, but then she nodded. "I'll be right outside if you need me." She dropped Lillian's hand and headed toward the door. She stopped when she got to Joshua. "If you do anything to upset her, I will hunt you down." She narrowed her eyes.

Joshua raised his hands and nodded. "Noted."

She gave him one more final glare and left.

The nurse stood there as if she didn't know what to do. Then she pushed the machine to the wall and backed away. "I'll come back in a few minutes. You have your call button, use it if you need anything."

Lillian thanked her and then waited until she heard the door click before she turned back to Joshua. Just as she opened her mouth to speak, another contraction came.

Once it peaked, she breathed out the tension and then turned to her snake ex-husband. "What do you want, Joshua? How did you even know I was here?"

He glanced around before he moved to the chair that Tamara had vacated. He sat on it, leaning forward and resting his elbows on his knees. "I've been following your engagement to Reed Williamson."

Panic raced through her chest. Was he here for money? "Well, that's not going to happen, so if you're here for money, forget it."

Joshua shook his head. "See, I knew that was the first thing you were going to think. That I was some money grubbing loser here to get money from his pregnant ex." He shook his head. "It's not like that. I just realized how much I missed you. It hurt me to see another man be with my wife. To be father to my baby." He nodded toward her stomach.

Out of instinct, Lillian brought her hand up to her stomach. She needed to protect this baby from Joshua. "The one you demanded I abort 'cause you didn't want a baby?"

A sheepish expression crossed his face. "I was scared,

Lil. I didn't know what I was doing. The first baby freaked me out. And then you got pregnant so fast"—he ran his hands through his hair—"I didn't know what to do."

Lillian swallowed. She knew that reaction all too well. Running because you were scared. But that still didn't excuse his behavior.

As if sensing her hesitation, he leaned over and grasped her hand. "I'm ready now, Lil. I want to be here for you and the baby. I want to be a family."

The last word fell from his lips and hung in the air. She studied him. A family was all she'd ever wanted. And one with Reed wasn't possible. Even if she didn't want Joshua in her life, how could she keep him from her baby's?

She took a deep breath and nodded. "Okay. If you want to be here for the baby, I can't stop you." She pulled her hand away and held it to her chest. "But know that you and I are finished. We can never be a couple." She narrowed her eyes. "Understand?"

A triumphant smile spread across his face. "Perfect," he said as he leaned back.

Lillian relaxed against her pillows as she breathed through another contraction. Tamara was not going to be happy when Lillian told her what she'd agreed to. But at this point, Lillian was so confused, she didn't know what she was doing. All she knew was that Reed was out of her life, and that pain hurt her more than allowing her ex back into it.

CHAPTER EIGHTEEN

Reed paced in his grandfather's study. It had been an hour since he'd put Lillian on that helicopter, and he was a mess. Every time he passed the windows that faced the back lawn, his gaze fell to the helicopter pad and the memory of Lillian in his arms rushed back to him. He could feel her against his chest as if she were there with him.

Growling, he rubbed his hands over his face. Why had he been such an idiot? What was wrong with him?

Pain took hold of his chest as the truth flooded his mind. It was because he loved her. She was everything to him and now she was gone. He'd tried to tell her, but she brushed him off as if he didn't matter. As if this marriage was only what it had been designed to be. A business contract between the two of them.

But it had become something more. He'd felt it, and he was sure Lillian had felt it as well.

She was just scared. Of what, he didn't know, but he had to find out. As he made his way to the door, a knock startled him. Pulling it open, he glanced down to see Cassie standing there with a determined look. He raised an eyebrow.

"Where are you going?" she asked as she took a step back and studied him.

Not wanting to waste time standing there, explaining himself to his sister, he tried to step past her. "I have a place to be," he said.

Cassie folded her arms and remained in his path. "You're an idiot," she said.

Reed hesitated as he glanced down at his sister. "What?"

"You let the most amazing girl slip through your grasp. There's only one explanation for that. You are an idiot." She emphasized her words with a jab to his chest.

Had she not been in the same room as him? "Cas, she told me not to come."

Cassie rolled her eyes. "And you listened? Clearly she wanted you there. No one wants to go to the hospital alone. Not when the person they love is on another island." She steeled her expression, as if that was going to intimidate him.

"Cas, I love that you are trying to be all protective, but I don't need it," he said, reaching out and pulling his kid sister into a hug.

She stiffened for a moment and then pulled back so she could look up at him. "You don't?"

Reed shook his head. "I'm going to the hospital. I realized that I need to be there even if she doesn't want me there. We're family and family members don't abandon each other."

A wide smile spread across her face. "Yeah, they don't." She reached out and wrapped her arms around his chest. He laughed as she squeezed him. "You're not as dumb as you look, big bro," she said, pulling away and punching his shoulder.

He pretended to wince and then smiled at her. "I'm happy," he said.

She patted his back. "Go get her."

Reed nodded and swallowed as he passed by. It was a half-hour boat ride to the mainland and then another thirty minutes to the hospital. He hoped she would be there when he arrived. And perhaps she would be excited to see him. But that might be pushing his luck.

WITH TRAFFIC, it took an hour longer then he'd planned. Ground travel was such a time suck. He walked through the sliding doors of the hospital and glanced around. A woman sat at the information desk, tapping on the keyboard in front of her. He swallowed as he approached.

He wasn't sure what he was going to say to her or how much information she could give away. But he was going to try to locate Lillian. It was the least he could do.

"Hello," he said, leaning against the counter.

The woman's bright green eyes met his and her jaw slacked. "You're Reed Williamson," she said, exhaling and letting her gaze roam over him.

It was strange to be recognized. But it made sense. Everything about his life this last week had been publicized. He put on his biggest grin. "I am." He leaned closer. "And I'm looking for someone."

She nodded as her fingernails clicked on the keys. "Lillian. I saw her get airlifted from your grandfather's home." She narrowed her eyes as she stuck out her finger and ran it along the screen of the monitor. "Ah, here she is."

Relief flooded his chest. "That's amazing. Can you tell me her room number?"

Her gaze made its way over to him as she raised her eyebrows. "We're really not supposed to do that."

Crap. But she knew him, and she knew that Lillian knew him. Perhaps, he could work some of his Williamson charm. "She's expecting me." He leaned closer and winked at her. "I'd forever be in your debt."

The woman rocked back in her chair and folded her arms. "For a hundred thousand dollars I'll tell you."

Reed raised his eyebrows. "What?"

The women's expression remained serious and then she broke into a smile. "I'm just joking. Lillian's in room 4B in Labor and Delivery."

Reed tapped the counter he'd been leaning on and nodded. "Thanks." And then he stopped and glanced back over at her. "Did you say Labor and Delivery?"

The receptionist nodded. "Yep. Straight up those elevators to the fourth floor. They'll guide you from there."

He knit his eyebrows. Why was Lillian in Labor and Delivery? Did they run out of room in the ER? As he walked down the hall, he saw a small gift shop. His thoughts turned to Lillian and what he was going to say when he got to her room. Suddenly, showing up empty-handed seemed like the worst idea.

So he beelined into the store. Flowers lined one wall, while helium balloons danced under the air vent above. Chocolates and stuffed animals filled the shelves. Reed stopped in front of a giant stuffed panda bear and studied it. Would Lillian like it? What did he know? Maybe?

After waffling for a few minutes, he grabbed it and brought it to the register. A woman was helping a guy who was buying a huge bouquet of roses. Reed tried not to eavesdrop but something caught his attention.

"Yep, a girl. We're so excited," the guy said as he handed the attendant his card.

She smiled. "That's amazing. Congrats." She took it and swiped it in the card reader next to the register.

The man nodded and turned, meeting Reed's gaze.

Reed raised his eyebrows. "Have a baby?"

The man shook his head. "Not yet. We had a scare, but everything seems settled down now. I just found out it's a girl." The man drummed his fingers on the counter as the woman swiped his card again. "We were split up for a while, but now we're back together. I have to convince her that she can't live without me," he said nodding toward the roses.

Reed nodded. Was it strange that this man was confessing this to him? Probably not. He seemed determined. Probably just working through his game plan by talking it out.

"Sir, I'm sorry, but your card keeps coming back declined." The attendant handed his card to him.

He took it and embarrassment passed over his face. "I'm sorry." He shuffled through his wallet. "Here. Try this." He handed another card over.

The woman ran it. After a few seconds, she shook her head and handed it back. "Sorry. Declined again."

The man took it and slipped it into his wallet. "I—"

Feeling sorry for the guy, Reed pulled out his card and handed it to the woman. "Ring both up," he said, nodding toward the bear and then the flowers.

A relieved expression passed over the man's face. "Geez, thanks," he said, clapping Reed on the shoulder.

Reed shook his head. "Don't mention it. The least I can do for someone who just received good news."

The man nodded and reached for the bouquet. "Lil will love this."

Reed stopped. What did he just say? "Who?"

The man smiled as if he knew what he'd just done. "Lil. Lillian? I'm Joshua, her husband."

Heat raced up Reed's spine. So he had heard right. He

took the pen from the attendant and signed the receipt she'd handed him. "You know Lillian?"

Joshua scoffed. "I know who you are. You're Reed Williamson." He folded his arms, holding the flowers so that they stuck straight up. "What are you doing here?" He glanced over at the bear. "Is that for her?"

Still trying to process just what was happening, Reed grabbed the bear and turned to study Joshua head on. "Are you here with another woman?" He felt thoroughly confused.

Joshua raised his eyebrows. "No. Lillian's pregnant with my baby." He let out a mocking laugh. "Did she not tell you?"

Lillian's pregnant? And she'd gone into labor. That was what had happened to her. Worry flowed through his mind as he made his way to the hall. Joshua was hot on his heels.

"Where are you going?"

"I need to talk to her."

A hand reached out and grabbed his elbow. Reed stopped and stared down at Joshua's hand. Why was he touching him? "Please remove your hand."

Joshua pulled back but kept his close proximity. "I just think we should talk about this first."

Reed shook his head. "See, that's where you are wrong. You may be the ex-husband, but I'm the current fiancé. I need to talk to her." He headed toward the elevator.

"She wants to be a family," Joshua called after him.

Reed stopped at that word. Family. The one thing that

Lillian wanted more than anything. He turned and studied Joshua who had a smug expression. He had known that would get him to hesitate. He sauntered up to Reed as if he knew he'd already won.

"She told me before we had the ultrasound that she wanted to try again. She wants to do it for the baby." He reached out and brushed Reed's shoulder. "Seems like she picked the better man." He met Reed's gaze and smiled. "If you'll excuse me, I'm going to go up to be with my wife and child." He side-stepped Reed and pressed the elevator button.

Frustration boiled up inside of him. There was no way he was going to let this snake win. He'd already lost one girl to an awful person; there was no way he was going to have that happen again. He would go up there and talk to Lillian. He wanted her to tell him that she didn't want him around. There was no way he was going to take her ex's word for it.

He waited outside the elevator until the doors opened. Joshua boarded and Reed followed. When he turned, Joshua raised his eyebrows.

"Where are you going?" he asked, pressing the button for the fourth floor.

"I'm going to talk to Lillian."

Anger raced across Joshua's face. "No, you're not."

There was no way this guy was going to intimidate him, when Reed was a foot taller and twice his size. "Yes. I am. She gets to tell me to leave, not you."

Joshua shrugged, studying the floor numbers as the elevator climbed. "Fine. I'll enjoy that better anyway."

They rode the rest of the way in silence. Reed focused on what he was going to say to Lillian. When the doors opened, revealing the Labor and Delivery desk, his confidence wavered.

What if she didn't want to see him? How much worse would it be to ride all the way up here, just to be rejected to his face?

He'd already had that happen once. Could he survive another heart break? But then he nodded. He could never live with himself if he walked away without telling Lillian how he felt.

He followed after Joshua, who strutted through the hall and stopped at room 4B. He winked at Reed as he pushed open the door, leading with the flowers.

"Where did you get those?" Lillian's voice came from inside the room.

Reed hesitated, gathering his courage. The familiarity of the sound of her voice washed over him, rendering him speechless. He missed her, even though it had only been a few hours since he'd seen her.

"There's someone to see you," Joshua said.

"Who?" she asked.

"You can come in. My *wife* is decent."

Reed heard Lillian scoff, and he'd hoped that it was because she'd been classified as Joshua's wife. But before she could answer, Reed stepped into the room.

Lillian's skin paled when her gaze fell on him. She straightened, pulling the blanket around her. "What are you doing here?" she asked, her gaze sweeping the room as if she expected the paparazzi to jump out from behind him and start shooting pictures.

"Lillian, you went to the hospital. What kind of friend would I be if I didn't come visit you?" He extended the bear to her.

Her expression softened as she took it. "Thanks."

He nodded and glanced around the room. A monitor was set up next to her. One was tracking her heartbeat and the other...her baby. It was true.

When his gaze found hers, she dropped it. As if her secret was dirty, and she was embarrassed that he'd found out.

"You're pregnant," he said and mentally slapped himself. Of course she was. Why did he have to state the obvious?

She chewed her lip and nodded. "I didn't know how to tell you," she whispered.

His heart squeezed. How scared she must have been this entire time. Hiding this secret like it was something terrible. It hurt that she'd felt she couldn't tell him. How terrible of a person was he to make her feel as if this was something she needed to hide.

"You could have told me," he said as he smiled at her. He wanted to tell her that everything was okay.

She chewed her lip as she studied him. "Thanks."

Joshua cleared his throat. "Well, isn't that nice. I'm happy that the two of you could talk." He stood and walked over, extending his hand toward the bear. "It was nice of you to bring this by." He shot Reed a triumphant smile. "Anything else you want to say to Lillian?"

Reed cleared his throat as he ran his gaze over Joshua. Man, he did not like this guy, but he was right. If Lillian was going to be happy, the best thing he could do was step aside. If all she had ever wanted was a family, then he wasn't going to stand in the way of it.

"I've decided to come clean to my grandfather and tell him about the contract. If he uses this as a reason for me not to be CEO, so be it. I've been contemplating the idea of starting my own company." It hurt to speak those words out loud, but he couldn't work for Mason if his grandfather decided to allow him to inherit. Besides, he was done with contractually binding a woman to marry him. The next time he fell in love, it would be for real.

When he met Lillian's gaze, his stomach sank. She looked so small and fragile. She was blinking as she nodded. "I understand." Then her lip quivered. "I'm sorry I disappointed you."

Reed took a step toward her, but Joshua beat him to it. He sat down on the bed next to Lillian and wrapped his arms around her, pulling her close. "I think you should go now," he said, narrowing his eyes at Reed.

Not wanting to stand there and break Lillian's heart anymore, he nodded and made his way out of her room and into the hall. He paused, leaning his back against the wall. He was fighting the pull to go back into the room and confess everything to her.

He wanted her to know that he loved her. That he didn't care about the contract. She was the person he was meant to be with. And her having a baby was just the whipped cream on top.

But it wasn't what she wanted. When she looked at him, all she would see was the contract she had signed to be with him. If she could make a family with her baby's father, then Reed wasn't going to stand in the way.

He pushed off the wall and made his way down the hall. When he stopped in front of the elevator, he heard someone call his name. For a moment, he allowed the hope that it was Lillian. But he groaned when he saw Joshua running to catch up to him.

When he stopped in front of Reed, he clasped his hands together. "This is a bit awkward, but Lillian wanted me to check with you to make sure you were still going to compensate her for her efforts." He shrugged. "After all, you're the one calling this all off."

Reed raised his eyebrows. Lillian wanted this? Of course. That was all women saw him as. A bank account. For some reason, it didn't quite feel right, but what did Reed know. He was beginning to think that he might not ever understand women.

"She will get what the contract said." He would be true to his word, even if she couldn't.

Joshua smiled. “Wonderful.”

The elevator doors opened, and Reed stepped into the car. As the door closed, Reed blew out his breath. He couldn’t believe that his relationship with Lillian was ending. It was done. Over. Well, he had dealt with one heartache already; he was a pro by now.

CHAPTER NINETEEN

LILLIAN SAT on the hospital bed two days later. She was dressed and ready to get the heck out of this place. She was tired of the constant nurses and doctors. And if she were honest with herself, she was tired of Joshua's insistence that he stay with her. She was ready for some space from him.

Plus, she was having a hard time forgetting Reed. Every time someone knocked on the door, her heart skipped a beat, hoping that it was Reed coming back to tell her that he was sorry—that he couldn't live without her. Which is what she had realized she couldn't do. She couldn't live without him.

But, he'd pulled away when he found out she was pregnant, just as she had feared. She'd broken his trust and she doubted that he would ever be able to forgive her. It was all her fault.

Joshua walked into the room and smiled at her. "Doc

says you're good to go," he said, grabbing her overnight bag that Tamara had brought and slung it over his shoulder.

She nodded and stood. The last thing she wanted to do was go anywhere with Joshua, but she couldn't go back to Reed's place, and her old apartment was already rented out. She needed a place to stay while she figured out just what she was going to do before the baby got here. Which could happen in the next month or so.

Her fingers found their way down to her stomach. She'd gotten attached to this little girl from all the ultrasounds they'd done on her. Lillian had been able to see her tiny toes and fingers and watch her heartbeat. She was very much alive, and Lillian had fallen in love with her.

Joshua led the way out of the room and down the hall. They boarded the elevator and rode it to the lobby. When they got to the front doors, Joshua held up his hand.

"I'll grab the car," he said, walking through the automatic doors and out to the parking lot.

Lillian nodded and sat on the bench just inside the doors. Her phone chimed, and she pulled it from her purse. It was a text from Persephanie, Reed's assistant.

Lillian's heart picked up speed as she clicked on it.

Reed would like to compensate you for your trouble. Please send me the routing number and bank account you would like the funds deposited into.

Lillian swallowed as she read the words. Seriously? Reed wanted to pay her? Had he not felt the same way she did? Tears stung her eyes as she scoffed and glanced up to the ceiling. She was such a fool. Reed didn't feel anything for her. It was all about the contract, and Reed didn't seem like the kind of guy to go back on his word.

Emotion took over and she typed how she felt.

Tell him no. I don't want to be paid. I didn't fulfill the contract, so he doesn't owe me anything.

She hit send and waited for a reply. It took what felt like ages before her phone chimed.

Okay. I will let him know.

And just like that, Reed was out of her life. She doubted he was even thinking about her. He'd probably already convinced his grandfather to will him the company without the stupid stipulation. She wasn't there to drag him down anymore. And if his grandfather decided to keep with the marriage requirement, she was sure Reed was going to do just fine on his own.

Without her.

"Lillian?"

Desiree's voice startled her. Lillian turned to see her contagious smile peering down at her. Without thinking, Lillian stood and wrapped her arms around Desiree. She couldn't believe how much she missed everyone. Desiree, Cassie, Harold, Bert. All these people who had become such a part of her life. People who Reed had so graciously shared with her.

Lillian saw them as family.

"Oh, sweetheart," Desiree said, returning the hug. "I heard what happened. Mr. Reed's been stomping around the flat all morning."

Lillian pulled back to study Desiree. "What are you doing here?"

Desiree motioned toward the bench, and they both sat down. She wrapped her hand over Lillian's. "My nephew, the dork. Tried to jump from a picnic table to a low hanging tree branch. Let's just say, he didn't make it. Now he's being seen for a cast." She rolled her eyes.

Lillian glanced around. "I'm sorry. Do you need to go to him?" She didn't want to inconvenience her.

Desiree shook her head and smiled. "No. His mom is with him. Besides, I want to talk to you. I've missed you. Reed. That man. I swear. He's a bear without you there." Her expression turned serious. "He'd never say it, but that man misses you. More than you know."

Lillian's heart soared. Was it true? She couldn't allow herself to believe it though. If she hoped, then her heart would break even more than it was right now. She decided to brush off her comment. "I'm sure he's just sad he didn't get the company."

Desiree shook her head. "He actually went to his grandfather and gave his blessing to Mason." Desiree laughed. "The old man suddenly realized how stupid the whole thing was and didn't want to lose Reed so he wrote it out of the will. Reed's CEO."

Lillian couldn't help but smile. She was happy for Reed. He deserved it.

When she glanced over at Desiree, she saw that she was studying her. Lillian quirked an eyebrow. "What?"

Desiree shrugged. "I just don't get it. Why did you run back to your ex-husband when you had such a good thing going with Reed? And don't say you don't care about him 'cause you're not that good of a liar."

Lillian's stomach twisted; what was she supposed to say to that? "Reed wanted out. I didn't want him to feel like it was his duty to stick around." Lillian waved toward her body. "I'm a mess and being with me would be messy."

Desiree folded her arms, tapping her finger on her arm. "Yeah. I can see that." Then she sighed and reached out, placing her hand on Lillian's shoulder. "But honey, love will always be messy. If you go into it thinking you're going to come out clean, you're just going to be let down. But our purpose in life is to find that person we want to be messy with."

"But... I'm pregnant." The words came out lower than a whisper. It was still hard to admit, even though she was pretty much in love with the little nugget growing inside her.

Desiree nodded. "Reed told me." She leaned forward and met Lillian's gaze. "Trust me, Reed's the one you want beside you through this. That man will love that baby more than you could know. He already does, and do you know why?"

Lillian's heart raced so fast, she could hear it in her ears. "Why?"

Desiree leaned back, taking her sweet time to answer. "'Cause he loves the momma. And that's all you need. Reed will never leave you. He's more loyal than a German Shepherd. He won't run at the first sign of stress. Unlike some people I know."

Lillian could only assume she meant Joshua. But Joshua was back and said he wanted to be part of the baby's life. She couldn't discredit that. "I don't know." Lillian couldn't think right now. Her mind was too mixed up.

Desiree reached out and patted her hand. "Well, Lillian, don't wait too long. That man will only wait around for a while. And trust me, he's one you don't want to lose."

Just as she finished speaking, Joshua walked through the sliding doors. His gaze fell on them and he gave her a quizzical look. Lillian straightened and waved to Desiree.

"This is Desiree, Reed's friend. Desiree, this is Joshua. He's my ex-husband."

Joshua reached out his hand. "Well, we're talking about the 'ex' part."

Desiree eyed him and then shook his hand. "It's nice to meet you, Joshua. You better know what you're doing with our Lillian here. That girl is family, and if you hurt her, you'll have a world of pain come down on you." She narrowed her eyes.

Lillian swallowed. She was family to Desiree. Something she'd wanted forever. And nothing had sounded so good.

"I'll keep that in mind," Joshua said, motioning toward Lillian. "We should get going."

Lillian nodded. She gave Desiree one more hug—and whispered that she'd call her—and then followed Joshua out the door and into his rattling Malibu. Once she was situated, he shut the door and rounded the hood.

He slid the car into drive and pulled out of the parking lot. Lillian leaned back in her seat but couldn't ignore the uncomfortable feeling that grew in her stomach. This wasn't right. What a stark contrast between sitting with Reed and sitting here with Joshua.

With Reed it was comfortable and easy. With Joshua, it was painful. All she could remember were the awful times they'd had together. How he broke her heart during the loss of their first baby and through pretty much this entire pregnancy.

Why had he even come back? Why did he suddenly want to be a part of her life?

Then realization dawned on her. The money. Why didn't she see it before? She was so desperate to have family in her life, she'd take back someone who treated her badly just to be close to someone. What a fool she'd been.

Determined to prove her theory, she turned to Joshua. "Funny thing. I just got a text from Reed's personal assistant."

Joshua glanced over at her. “Oh, really? What did she say?”

Lillian shrugged, hoping to come across as relaxed. “She wanted to know where to send the money from Reed.”

Joshua’s grip tightened on the wheel. “And?”

Lillian brushed her skirt down. “I told her not to send it. I didn’t feel right keeping it. Besides, you’re here and can help me take care of the baby.”

Joshua whipped his gaze over to her. “Why did you say that? Are you an idiot?”

He slammed on his brakes as he stopped at the traffic light. Lillian had to brace herself with her hand on the dashboard. She glared at him.

“What was that about? Do you want to hurt me? The baby?” She wrapped her arm around her waist out of instinct.

Joshua ran his hand through his hair. “You call her back. You tell her right now, you want that money.” His eyes were wild as he glanced around. He must have seen her reaction because his face softened. “I mean, we need that money, hun. For the baby.” He reached out to touch her stomach, but Lillian slapped his hand away.

“How dare you,” she said, narrowing her eyes. “You are a snake and will only ever be a snake. You came in talking about how you want a part of this baby’s life. I should have known better. You just saw it as an opportunity for a quick buck.” She folded her arms. “That’s all I ever was to you. I wasn't your family. I was someone you could use and cast aside."

Shouldering her purse, she pulled on the door handle and climbed out of the car. Horns were honking behind them as the light turned green.

Rain started to fall around her, but Lillian didn't care. She wasn't getting back into the car with that jerk. He was officially out of her life for good.

"Get back in the car, Lil," Joshua said, leaning over the seat and motioning to her.

Lillian turned and waited for an opening in traffic.

"Get in the car, Lillian," Joshua said, this time with much more aggression.

"Good bye, Joshua," she said, taking the break of cars as her opportunity to race across the street. Joshua yelled some profanity and something else about her missing out, and then sped away.

Now alone, she wrapped her arms around her chest and looked around. She really wasn't sure what she was going to do now. The only thought that entered her mind involved Reed—and how much she wanted to see him right now. She groaned. She'd left her phone in Joshua's car, and she was pretty sure he wasn't going to bring it back to her. Determined to not let that derail her, she studied the people walking by.

A portly man with an umbrella caught her eye. She reached out her hand and touched his shoulder.

"Excuse me, sir. Do you have a phone I could borrow?"

The man stopped and looked her up and down. He must have taken pity on her because he reached into his suit coat and handed one over. “Make it quick,” he said.

Lillian nodded as she dialed Reed’s number.

It took four rings for him to answer.

“Hello?”

Butterflies erupted in Lillian’s stomach. His voice was so familiar. The cadence caused shivers to race across her skin. At this moment, all she wanted to do was see him.

“Hey, Reed.”

There was silence on the other end.

“Lillian? Whose phone are you calling me from?”

She glanced over at the balding man who raised his eyebrows as if to signify he was running out of patience. “A really nice man on the side of the street.”

He scoffed and motioned for her to finish up.

Reed cleared his throat. “Where’s Joshua?”

Lillian chewed her lip. “He’s...gone.”

“Gone?”

She closed her eyes, praying that he’d go along with what she was asking. “Can you come get me?”

More silence. “Where are you?”

After giving him the cross streets, Reed said he’d be there in a few minutes and hung up. The man took his phone and left her standing there, in the rain.

Now alone, she had time to regret just what she’d done. Why had she called Reed? What was she going to say to him? She shivered as she pushed herself farther under the building behind her. Fearing that Reed wouldn't find her if she left to find more shelter, she stayed.

Finally, his car pulled up to the sidewalk and he jumped out. Running over to her, his gaze ran over her. "What are you doing out in the rain?" he asked, shrugging off his coat and lifting it over her head.

"I had to talk to you." She glanced up at him, hoping he'd see just what she was trying to say.

He hesitated, meeting her gaze. "What about?"

"I didn't take the money," she blurted out.

Water dripped off Reed's hair as he continued to study her. She probably looked like a drowned rat, but she wasn't going to move. She had Reed right where she wanted him and there was no way she was going to let this moment pass. She was going to tell him just how she felt.

"Why?" he asked.

She stepped closer to him, judging his reaction. He didn't move to get away from her which she took as a good sign.

"Because it didn't feel right. To me, there was no more contract." She took another step toward him. "Because I fell in love with you." She raised her gaze to meet his. What she saw took her breath away.

Reed's forehead was furrowed as he studied her. As if he were trying to digest the information.

"Reed, I love you," she repeated. Why wasn't he saying anything?

He ran his hand through his hair as he glanced to the

side. She watched as he squinted. Then he turned to look at her. "Are you sure?" He looked hopeful but also nervous. As if she held the fate of his heart in her hands.

She stepped up to him this time, closing the gap between their bodies. She reached out and rested her hands on his chest. She could feel his pounding heart against her hands. Relief flooded her body. He was just as nervous as she was. When she peeked up at him, she saw that his expression had turned serious.

"I loved you from the moment I saw you standing in your little apartment." He bent closer to her, his lips hovering just above hers.

That what just what she needed to hear. She lifted herself up onto her toes and pressed her lips against his. Fireworks exploded through her body as he wrapped his arms around her and drew her in close. She slid her hands up his shoulders and to his neck, where she entwined her fingers.

When they pulled apart, he glanced down. Suddenly, a sheepish expression passed over his face as he reached out and pressed his hand against her stomach.

"Am I hurting the baby?"

She shook her head. "Nope. The baby is just fine."

He looked relieved. "It's a girl?"

Lillian bit her lip. "Yes." She studied him, not sure how he was going to react.

He moved his hand to cup her cheek. Then he kissed her forehead, nose and then lips. "Marry me?" he asked.

She pulled back to look at him. "What?"

He leaned closer, pressing his forehead against hers. "Marry me. Make a family with me."

That was all she needed to hear. Throwing away all her fears and doubts, Lillian wrapped her arms around him and pulled him close. She was finally getting everything she'd ever wanted. Reed was hers and she was never going to let him go.

EPILOGUE

The early morning light crept in between the drapes that were pulled shut. Reed shifted, reaching out to feel for Lillian. As always, her side of the bed was empty. He smiled as he heard the whir of the pottery wheel across the hall. Lying on his back, he stared up at the ceiling.

Cooing broke into his thoughts. He turned to focus on the bassinet beside the bed. He'd insisted that Cora sleep right next to him. Lillian had protested, but finally gave in.

Sitting up, he peeked in at his daughter. Four months old and more beautiful than anything he'd ever seen. Her wide, blue eyes peered back at him.

"How's daddy's princess?" he asked, picking her up and pulling her to his chest.

She wiggled in his embrace before letting out a tiny whine. He shushed her as he made his way across the hall.

Lillian was at her pottery wheel. She had on her cut-off

shorts and a tank. Dried clay was smeared across her skin. She jumped when he moved into view.

A smile spread across her lips as her gaze made its way from his face to Cora.

"She woke up?" she asked.

He pulled Cora from his shoulder and glanced down at her. "Eh, it wasn't anything daddy couldn't handle." Cora made a small squeak, so Reed brought her back up to his shoulder.

"How's it coming?" he asked, nodding toward the vase she was making.

Lillian used her wrist to push back some loose hair. A content expression passed over her face. "It's getting there," she said, standing and moving away from the wheel.

He followed her out of the room and over to the huge picture windows that overlooked the ocean. They were spending some much-needed time at the house in the Hamptons. His grandfather had passed away a month ago and he'd been thrown into the full responsibilities of CEO.

Making sure to put his family first, he suggested that his two girls go with him for a week away. Lillian had jumped at the opportunity.

"Here, let me take her. You"—she nodded at him —"make your starving wife some of your famous eggs."

He laughed, handing her Cora. When his daughter was safely in her arms, he pulled them both close, and pressed his lips against Lillian's. A satisfied feeling settled in his stomach. This was exactly where he needed to be. These women were his family. And he was never going to let them go.

"I love you, Mrs. Williamson. No contract needed."

She pulled back, staring up at him with her bright blue eyes. "I love you, Mr. Williamson." Then she leaned forward. "Now feed me before I starve."

***

Want MORE romance?

Grab **The Engagement with the Prince**!!

A broken hearted nurse and a prince desperate to live the life that he wants, decide to fake a relationship.

They just didn't expect the feelings that grew.

Grab it from Amazon HERE!

Do you LOVE Audiobooks?

Check out Anne-Marie/Marie Meyer's YouTube channel where you can listen to her stories for FREE!

Just make sure you subscribe so you get all notifications!

HERE

JOIN THE NEWSLETTER

Want to learn about all of Anne-Marie Meyer's new releases plus amazing deals from other authors?
Sign up for her newsletter today and get deals and giveaways!
PLUS a free novella, Love Under Contract

TAKE ME TO MY FREE NOVELLA!

Anne-Marie Meyer lives in MN with her husband, four boys, and baby girl. She loves romantic movies and believes that there is a FRIENDS quote for just about every aspect of life.

Connect with Anne-Marie on these platforms!

anne-mariemeyer.com

www.facebook.com/authorannemariemeyer

Printed in Great Britain
by Amazon